A Mother's Sins

*To Phyllis
Happy reading
Ursula T...*

A novel by
Ursula Turner

Ursula Turner

This book is a work of fiction. Names, characters, places, and incidents either are the product of the author's imagination or, are used fictitiously. Any resemblance to actual events, locales, or persons, living or dead, is entirely coincidental.

All rights reserved including the right or reproduction

ISBN: 0-9764666-9-4

Cover Art by: Sylvia Rutledge

Cover by: Krystal Neuhofel

1110 West 5th Street
Coffeyville, Kansas 67337
www.tanosbookspublishing.com

Printed in the United States of America

A Mother's Sins

Dedication

To my husband, Jack, who never complained as I sat at my computer night after night, and whose patience made this book possible.

Ursula Turner

A Mother's Sins

Chapter 1

The beat-up looking little car groaned ominously when Holly's foot pressed the gas pedal almost to the floor. Although the road wound its way up a gentle incline, the ancient vehicle struggled forward.

"Come on, Betsy," Holly whispered, gently patting the dashboard in front of her, "Sure, you're getting on in years, but I know you can make it. Just a little farther and we'll be there."

If mother could only hear me, Holly thought, she would think I'm losing my mind talking to a car as though it were a person. Besides, having been alone so much Holly had gotten into the habit of talking to herself as well. So, she reasoned, talking to a car did not seem all that bad. In addition, the car was all she had left of her mother's possessions besides a few small mementoes, and it was very dear to her. She'd had to sell everything else to pay the mountains of medical bills left over from her mother's illness. The insurance hadn't come near to covering all of the debts.

But Holly didn't want to think about that now. It made her feel so sad, and it was much too beautiful a day to think about anything as depressing as her mother's illness and subsequent death.

The road she was traveling on was lined with apple trees that were in full bloom. The intoxicating aroma of the blossoms wafting through the open car windows was far superior to any expensive perfume, Holly decided.

An array of wildflowers, showing off in all the colors of the rainbow, peeked through the lush, green grass that covered the slightly hilly meadows. The view was so breathtaking, so spectacular, that Holly was finding it difficult to concentrate on her driving. Perhaps it was just as well that the old car couldn't move any faster. It also helped that there wasn't much traffic on this country road.

Holly knew it couldn't be much longer before she reached Seven Oaks, the manor house belonging to Senator VanDorn. She had studied the map thoroughly during the last few weeks and while doing so, had asked herself what this part of the country might look like. She had to admit that she was not at all disappointed with her first impression. She was actually looking forward to living here.

"I wonder if I will find what I am looking for?" Holly asked herself.

It hadn't been at all difficult for her to leave her hometown. After all, there had been nothing left to hold her there after her mother died. Martha Snyder had been quite ill for some time, an illness that had turned out to be terminal.

"There is nothing more I can do for her," the doctor had told Holly. "We can either place her in a nursing home, or you can take care of her at home. There isn't any reason she should have to stay in the hospital."

Holly had taken her mother home and had nursed her as best she could as the sickness progressed, taking care of her every need during endless days and many nights as well, watching her become more and more feeble and frail. She was frustrated by the knowledge that she didn't have the power to help this woman she loved so much. All she was able to do was to make her as comfortable as possible.

It came as no surprise to Holly that her friends stopped dropping by and that she eventually lost all contact with them, especially after she'd had to quit her job. But she had shouldered the heavy burden without complaint.

She had known all along that her mother could not win the battle against her illness. Nevertheless, she had not given up hope until the very end. That's why it had been such a shock to Holly when she'd entered her mother's bedroom one morning and discovered that she was no longer breathing. She had not wanted to believe that this woman, to whom she had always felt so close, was now dead -- gone from her forever.

What had bothered the young woman most was the fact that her mother had to die all by herself and she, Holly, had not spent the last hours or even minutes at her side.

"There is no reason to feel guilty," the doctor had assured her over and over. "Your mother went to sleep quietly. You probably wouldn't have noticed it had you been sitting right next to her."

But Holly had been unable, at first, to shake the feeling of guilt.

Then she had experienced another, even bigger shock than her mother's death had been, which she had known would come sooner or later. Immediately after the funeral, when she was sorting through her mother's papers, she'd discovered something totally unexpected. She hadn't been looking for anything specific, had only opened the safe and taken out the papers to be doing something to keep herself occupied, to keep her mind off the fresh pain of her loss. Had there been somebody there to talk to, she might not have thought of opening the safe for days, weeks even but, as throughout her mother's illness, she'd been alone in this. There had been no one to turn to. So she decided that keeping busy might lessen the ache in her heart and, touching her mother's things had, indeed, made her feel close to her. However, while in the process of looking through the stack of documents, she had found something that had upset her almost as much as had the death of her mother. The man, whom she had called daddy, had not been her biological father.

Bill Snyder had married Martha two years after Holly's birth and had then adopted the little girl. Holly remembered him as a dear, friendly man who had truly loved his little bumblebee, as he had called Holly. But, this man whom she had thought to be her father was no longer around either, having died seven years ago, and now there was no one Holly could ask about the adoption and who her birth father was. There were no other relatives to the best of Holly's knowledge.

"What am I supposed to think about all this?" Holly had said to her mirror image in the bathroom later that day, "I've got to do something to find out who I am."

It was difficult for her to believe that her mother had taken this kind of a secret with her to her grave, without a word, without even as much as a hint about this part of her past. Holly had been so shaken by the discovery, that she had stuffed all the papers back into the small safe and kept them locked up there for several days without looking at them again. But she couldn't stop thinking about this revelation and had continued to wonder and puzzle about who her real father might be.

"Who was this man?" she asked herself again and again. "To whom can I turn to find this part of my roots?"

Eventually Holly had realized that the only chance she would have of getting an answer to her questions would be to continue studying her mother's papers. She proceeded to examine them systematically this time, and by meticulously combing through them one by one, it came to her attention that one name kept coming up that was puzzling to her; puzzling, because the name was that of Senator Drew VanDorn, a well-known political figure. He was not someone she thought her mother would have known. And again he was not someone who was likely to be acquainted with her mother. However, until Holly had turned two, this man had sent money to Martha Snyder on a regular basis. The payments had stopped at the time of Holly's adoption.

Was the senator her father? The signs all pointed in that direction, although she could not imagine what such a famous man and her mother would have had in common.

There were so many questions and nobody from whom she could get answers.

Had it simply been a short affair between her mother and the senator? Knowing her mother, Holly couldn't bring herself to believe that of her. Perhaps the senator had been married. Or he had been too conceited to marry a woman who, with only a middle class background, he might have felt to be below him.

Whether it was coincidence or destiny, whatever one might call it, the very next day after discovering the VanDorn name in her mother's safe, while looking through the classified ads for a now badly needed job, she read to her amazement that Senator Drew VanDorn was looking for a personal secretary.

Holly had answered the ad immediately, giving herself no time to think it over and possibly change her mind. She had to try and get to know this man who might be her father, yet, at this point in time; she didn't want him to know what she suspected. That would come later. Right now she could only hope that he didn't know her adopted name and possibly recognize her through it, although, perhaps that might be the best outcome for her. That way she would know the answer for which she was searching.

During the next few days Holly tried to imagine this man who might well be her birth father. She drew a picture of him in her mind that did not show him in the best of light. She somehow saw him as a vain, snobbish individual from the upper class, too proud and conceited to associate with ordinary humans.

Two weeks after she'd applied for the job, the senator had called personally. To her surprise, the deep, friendly voice did not at all match the picture of him that she'd dreamed up. He had asked a few questions, and then had informed her that, due to the excellent references that had accompanied her application, he had decided to offer her the job. She was to report to his manor house, where she would be working and living. She would be starting her duties on the first day of the following month.

"My office is a mess," he said, "and I need someone who can start as soon as possible to get things straightened out."

Holly had been anxious to start her new job. The sooner she began, the quicker she would get the answers she was looking for, or so she hoped.

She slammed her foot on the brake hard, causing the little car to shudder. She'd almost missed the turn-off to her new place of employment that was to be her home as well. She had spotted the small, weathered sign just in the nick of time. Following the wide, meandering driveway slowly, not sure what to expect, she assumed that it couldn't be too much farther when she spotted the tops of several tall oak trees.

And then, around the next bend, the house came into view. Holly stopped the car and got out to let this first impression seep into her consciousness slowly. A little farther on, the driveway divided and led to the left and right around a fairly large pond, bordered by six -- not seven -- oak trees. Why the name "Seven Oaks?" She wondered. She would have to inquire about that later on. Right now she had better drive up the last small hill to the front of the house.

However, when she tried to start her car, it refused to respond. It had given all it was capable of giving and, without some serious attention, evidently wouldn't budge another inch. Holly wasn't surprised. In fact, it was a miracle that the old car had made it this far. She sighed and then decided that things could be worse. At least she was in sight of her destination, although it would be embarrassing to arrive on foot and have to explain why. She reached for her purse, deciding to leave the suitcases in the car for now, and this time she gave the fender a small pat, "I forgive you, Betsy," she said with a small smile. "You gave it all you had."

Chapter 2

Being forced to walk gave Holly a much better chance to get a good look at the place she might be calling her home for a while. Having lived in the city all of her life, she viewed this house as an enchanted castle, and then she wasn't even sure if she could call this a house. Mansion or manor might be a better word, Holly thought. Huge, white columns supported a large balcony, located above the wide marble entrance stairs. Scarlet colored, climbing roses had been planted in flower boxes along the edge of the balcony and they, along with their vivid green leaves almost hid its white, wrought iron railing. The house was pure, snowy white with the trim painted a pale pink. Holly didn't have much knowledge about architecture, but she could tell that this house had received several additions since it was first built, with each addition blending well into the total of the building. The mansion looked as though it was well kept -- no peeling paint here. There was no doubt that a woman had a hand in decorating it. Holly did not think a man would have chosen those colors, particularly the pink. The whole picture was pleasing to the eye, a woman's eye at any rate, Holly thought. She couldn't wait to meet the lady of the house.

As she stood there, taking it all in, Holly couldn't help but think of her mother. Had she ever stood here, looking longingly at the house, hoping to catch a glimpse of the man whom she loved so desperately? Holly couldn't quite put that picture together with the image she'd dreamed up of the man who'd hired her. She couldn't imagine that this man who had talked to her on the phone was the kind of person who would have abandoned the mother of his child as well as that child. It also wasn't likely that a man, who'd been thoughtful enough to send them money on a regular basis, could be that cruel.

With a sigh, Holly continued walking toward the building. What was the use? She told herself in exasperation; it was all nothing but guesswork at this point. She hoped sincerely that she would find the truth about her past in this house. She didn't know how she would be able to continue functioning without knowing who her real father was or had been.

When she saw the shiny, black limousine with its tinted windows standing next to the little red sports car, both vehicles parked in the curved driveway, she was almost glad that she didn't have to park her shabby little car next to all that elegance. That would certainly have been more embarrassing than to arrive on foot. But old Betsy was all she'd been able to afford to keep after paying off her mother's hospital bills. Besides, nobody had wanted to buy the ugly old thing. The house was gone, of course; there had been no other way for her to take care of those bills. And now she had the satisfaction of knowing that she didn't owe even one penny to anyone.

She'd made it halfway up the broad stairs when a stylishly dressed woman, a little past her middle years, opened the door. When Holly introduced herself, a friendly smile appeared on the face that had initially looked a little forbidding. Offering Holly a slender hand, the handshake was firm. She was quickly made aware that this pleasant woman was not the lady of the house as Holly had assumed.

"My name is Gertrude Walters," she said. "Sorry, I don't usually greet people so abruptly, but I didn't hear a car and wondered how you had made your way here. These days one can't be too careful, don't you agree? How did you get here? Oh, by the way, I'm the senator's housekeeper here at the manor."

After Holly had explained about her car's breakdown, and Gertrude Walters had assured her that it would be taken care of, the older woman led the newcomer toward the senator's offices which were located in the west wing. This was a somewhat newer and more male oriented addition to the building, as Holly noticed immediately. To reach this part of the manor, Gertrude had led her along so many hallways and passages and around corners of the older part of the building that Holly wondered if she would ever be able to find the way by herself

As though reading her mind, Gertrude laughed, "I know what you are thinking. I had a hard time finding my way around this house, too, when I first came here. But I learned quickly, and so will you."

Soon they arrived at a heavy, oaken door, which the housekeeper opened. The office behind the door was, with its modern furniture, a total contrast to the somewhat old-fashioned style of the earlier part of Seven Oaks, the part that the two women had traversed to get here. The high windows allowed lots of light to enter the room, besides giving out on a wonderful view of the perfectly manicured grounds surrounding the manor house, grounds that could almost be called a park. However, the oaks were not visible from this side of the building. A desk was positioned directly in front of one of the windows. Next to the computer that sat on one side of the desk, documents, papers and some unopened mail was piled high, threatening to topple over. This was without a doubt the work Holly had been hired to take care of. She hoped she would be able to handle that much all at once. It might be difficult since she was not familiar with the senator's businesses.

Between tall file cabinets, another door was visible.

"The room we're standing in will be your office," the housekeeper told her. "Behind that door," she pointed, "you'll find the senator's office, and we might as well go see him now, since he is, no doubt, expecting you."

Gertrude Walters rapped on the door once, then,

without waiting for an answer, stuck her head into the other room to announce Holly to the senator. Holly heard him invite the two of them to enter his office.

He had risen from his chair and was standing behind his desk before Holly had a chance to approach him. He studied her silently for some time. Seemingly liking what he saw, he came out from behind his desk, his hand stretched out toward her.

"Miss Snyder, I'm happy to be able to welcome you to Seven Oaks."

"Thank you, sir," Holly shook his offered hand, studying this tall man as he had studied her moments ago. She was looking for some kind of resemblance between him and herself, looking closely at his features to discover something, anything that might look familiar to her that might indicate a relationship between the two of them. There was nothing as far as she was able to determine.

The senator, who was past sixty, was slim, almost to the point of looking gaunt. His thick hair was snowy white. His age did not hide the fact that he had been handsome as a younger man. In fact, he was still quite attractive.

His slate gray suit fit perfectly, an indication that it had been made by an excellent tailor. A black tie patterned with tiny gray triangles, and black shoes that must have been freshly polished just this morning, completed the picture of a successful man.

Holly was glad she had chosen to wear her navy blue suit, the one giving her the look of a serious businesswoman. She had almost worn her more comfortable jeans and a t-shirt for the long drive. She would have felt much underdressed at this moment, had she done so.

The senator hadn't said a word while Holly had been looking him over. Now he smiled. "I hope I meet with your approval," he said with a twinkle in his eyes.

Holly blushed. "I'm sorry, sir," she managed to say after an awkward moment, "I didn't realize I was staring."

"As I was able to determine, you have excellent credentials," the senator overlooked her embarrassment. "That was the main reason I chose you for this position. But I must admit I'm happy to discover that my new secretary is very pretty as well."

Holly blushed for the second time within a few minutes, even though for a totally different reason. It was pleasant to receive such a nice compliment from a man, even if he was older. She was no longer used to male conversations after the months she'd spent almost exclusively at her mother's sickbed.

"As I told you on the phone," she explained, "I haven't worked for almost a year and am probably somewhat rusty." Holly found it necessary to mention this fact again because she wanted to be honest. She'd actually been surprised that this flaw in her resume hadn't counted against her.

The senator shook his head as he listened to her, "No need to worry about that. I took that into consideration," he said in his deep, confidence-inspiring voice. "I'm certain you'll catch on quickly. Besides, I find it admirable that you took care of your sick mother yourself instead of sending her to a nursing home, the way so many people do these days. In my opinion that's another plus for you. It shows that you are reliable and can be depended upon."

This was the third time that this man had caused Holly to blush. She hadn't received this much praise since she'd been a little girl and had come home from school with her grade card full of As.

But his approval of her wasn't the only reason that she would have found it impossible not to like this man. The friendly, open way with which he had approached her, a total stranger, as well as the hearty manner he expressed himself, made him instantly likable as far as Holly was concerned.

Drew VanDorn accompanied her to the outer office and looked around. "I know it's a little untidy in here right now, but I know you'll take care of that in no time, and I hope you'll like it here."

"I'm sure of it," Holly answered without hesitating even for one moment. She pointed to the piled up documents on the desk. "I suppose I should start right away. If I dig in now, I can learn what kind of work I'll be doing."

The senator laughed out loud, "I won't hear of it," he chuckled. "You've barely arrived. You'll have plenty of opportunity to begin learning the ropes tomorrow. For now, I suggest, you rest a little after your long drive. If you really insist on it, you can look around a little, but," he laughingly shook his finger at her, "no work yet. I do hope, however, that you won't be angry with me for not showing you around. I have a very important appointment in a few minutes."

The senator then called Mrs. Walters who had remained in the senator's office while the other two had been talking, and told her that Holly was ready to be shown to her living quarters.

"I'll see you at dinner," he promised.

A Mother's Sins

Chapter 3

Holly was surprised to find that, instead of the one room she had expected, she had been given an entire suite to spend her evenings and nights in.

The living room was furnished in delicate, pale pastels. It was almost as though she'd been expected and they had known that she loved pale colors. She was already looking forward to spending her evenings curled up on the chintz-covered sofa reading a good book, or to just relax there and daydream, with a glass of sweet wine, the kind she normally preferred, on the coffee table in front of her. The bedroom was kept equally light with the colors running mostly to white and pink, with a splash of burgundy repeated on throw pillows, on the curtain sashes, and on a strip of wallpaper just under the ceiling. The darker color, Holly thought, did give the room some substance. The canopy bed was enchanting. Not even as a little girl had Holly ever dreamed she'd be lucky enough to be able to sleep like the princess she'd read about in fairy tales, who she had then thought deserved such a bed. Now she couldn't keep her eyes off it. Gauzy white curtains featuring tiny pink polka dots enclosed it completely. When she pulled them aside, fluffy pillows and a down comforter, also covered with pink polka dots, revealed themselves -- a cozy place to spend ones nights, Holly reflected; a bed to ride out stormy nights and slumber deeply during calms ones.

A large, modern bathroom complemented the suite. Like the other rooms, it, too, had been kept light in its coloring with white tiles covering the walls and floor, and gilded faucets adorning the white marble sink and tub.

Holly couldn't believe that the rooms weren't dark and dank, the way she had imagined them when she had first pictured the manor. She had read somewhere that Senator VanDorn's mansion was supposed to be quite old. Then she remembered that, through the years, several owners had added on to the original building. Her suite must be located in one of the newer parts of this big house.

While Holly had been inspecting her new living quarters, Gertrude had been standing to one side, quietly watching as the young woman went from room to room, scrutinizing everything from the sofa to the bed and finally, the tub. She couldn't help but notice when Holly glanced longingly at the latter. She suppressed a loud laugh at the look on the young woman's face when she discovered the huge bathtub.

"Why don't you go ahead and run some hot water," the housekeeper smiled. "I'll send someone to your car for your luggage so you'll have a change of clothing waiting for you."

Holly, who was starting to feel the effects of her long trip, gave the other woman a grateful look. She handed her keys to the car, and, without hesitation, started to run some bath water, testing it to make sure the temperature was just right to soothe her weary body.

Before getting in, she looked around the spacious bathroom and opened some of the cabinet doors. Everything she would need for a luxurious bath had been provided. She discovered huge, fluffy, pink and white towels and matching wash cloths. There were several kinds of soap. Even bath oil had been provided, and she did not hesitate to pour some into the bath water. In one cupboard she found shampoo and conditioner. It was somewhat awe inspiring to Holly that it turned out to be her brand, the one she normally used. Coincidence? The hairdryer she'd found would certainly come in handy. Hers had conked out on her shortly before she'd left home, and she hadn't had a chance to replace it yet.

By the time she had gathered up everything she

would need, the tub was full, almost to overflowing, and the fragrant aroma of the bath oil filled the room. She climbed in, carefully testing the temperature once more to make sure she hadn't allowed it to get too hot. Sliding down slowly into the sudsy water, she leaned her head back and relaxed, closing her eyes.

Gertrude was descending the stairs, returning from showing Holly her rooms, when the senator rushed past her on his way to his appointment. When he saw her, he stopped, even though he was already running late.

"Well, how do you like Miss Snyder?" he inquired.

The housekeeper didn't take long with her answer, "She seems to be a likable young woman," she replied with a smile. Then her smile vanished and she became serious, "But hadn't you better take it easy before you succeed in making yourself sick? You know the doctor told you not to work so hard. Isn't that why you hired Miss Snyder? And rushing around like you're doing right now certainly won't improve your physical condition."

"Nonsense," Senator VanDorn usually valued Gertrude's opinion until she started to nag him about his health. But he was glad she agreed with him as far as Holly was concerned. She had, through her many years of running the house for him, proved repeatedly that he could trust her completely. At times he almost felt that the housekeeper had a sixth sense when it came to certain issues. Sometimes he almost felt that she knew him better than he knew himself, which was one of the reasons he didn't want her to say anything as far as his health was concerned. The main reason was that he feared she might be right, something he hesitated to admit, to himself, and most certainly to business acquaintances. But he had to admit, he had not been feeling his best lately. Well, he thought, with Holly here to help him, he might be able to take things somewhat easier, once he'd had the opportunity to show her the ropes.

Gertrude Walters was indeed able to read him,

because she looked at him now with worry in her eyes. What others didn't see, she noticed immediately -- the dark smudges under his eyes, the tired droop of his mouth, the effort it cost him to keep himself erect. Drew VanDorn couldn't fool her. She knew he wasn't feeling well, even if he tried not to show it. She'd been worrying about him for some time.

"You should rest a little," she told him now, with a hint of reproach in her voice, "instead of running all over creation."

VanDorn's response was to laugh, "Soon," he promised. "As soon as the senate closes for this session, I'll take a few days off."

"Am I really to believe that?" the housekeeper sighed. "If I know you at all, you'll be out getting votes, instead."

VanDorn laughed even louder, "Mrs. Walters, as long as you've been at Seven Oaks, I would have thought you'd know by now that I don't go after votes unless it's an election year. Besides," his face turned serious, "I've been thinking of calling it quits. I'm either getting too old or too tired for this business. Politics doesn't seem to have the edge it used to hold for me. Lately I've been tempted to spend more of my time running some of my other businesses, particularly this farm we're living on, and I would love to go to our other farm, the one in Texas. That is definitely something I intend to do in the near future. I haven't been there for a visit in a long time and would like to see how the place is shaping up. I know Olson is a good manager, but it never hurts to look after things yourself once in a while." He glanced at his watch again, noting how late he was already for his appointment. He really did not want to make the congressman he was supposed to be meeting wait any longer than necessary.

Gertrude Walters followed the tall figure with her eyes as he rushed along the lower hallway toward the entrance doors. She loved this man, had loved him since she'd first laid eyes on him, even though she knew that he would never return her feelings, that he regarded her only as a valued employee. She was well aware that the senator still mourned for his wife, even though she'd died years ago.

But the housekeeper was willing to settle for whatever little scraps he would subconsciously throw her way. Her own husband had died in a farm accident, a long time ago, and since she loved the country, her job as housekeeper for the senator seemed heaven-sent, since it had kept her from having to move to the city and find a job there. In addition, it allowed her to remain in close proximity to the senator. Although she knew this was all she would ever have, it was enough for her to be able to be there for him when he needed her. And she was happy when he shared his problems with her, because it proved to her that she was more to him than a mere employee.

She stood a while longer, deep in thought, still seeing him in her mind's eye, long after he was out of sight. At last she remembered that Holly was waiting for her suitcases, and she turned in the opposite direction the senator had taken, toward the back of the house, to find someone who would go to the car and bring Holly's luggage to her rooms.

Ursula Turner

Chapter 4

When Holly got out of the bathtub, she felt like a new person. Refreshed from the hot soak, she reached for the big, fluffy towel she'd laid out earlier and wrapped it around herself. Then she walked into the bedroom, where she found her suitcases waiting for her as promised. One had been placed on a small stand made especially for that purpose; the other was on the bed. Both had been opened, ready for her to take out what she might need. Holly was glad that, whoever had brought them, had not unpacked them. She was a private young woman and would have felt odd knowing a stranger had looked through her things.

For a change of clothing she opted, this time, to wear the jeans she'd rejected for the trip to her new place of employment. A bright red t-shirt and a pair of white joggers completed her outfit. She decided she'd unpack the rest of her things later. It was such a beautiful day that she did not want to waste another minute indoors. She'd had her fill of that while taking care of her mother. As much as she had loved that dear woman, it was hard, at times, not to be able to go for a walk now and then. Also, she was anxious to explore the grounds. Her clothes certainly wouldn't get any more wrinkled while waiting to be unpacked than they already were.

Holly had no patience with the blow dryer. It was taking much too long to finish its job on her hair. She pulled a red ribbon out of her cosmetics bag and used it to tie her shoulder-length, blond curls into a ponytail. There, she said to herself, that should do it. I think this will look fine for a stroll on the grounds. Wearing the jeans and t-shirt would surely be all right for what she had in mind.

She'd change again for dinner, but for the purpose of walking along the garden paths and under the trees she'd seen from her window, the clothes she'd chosen along with her joggers would be much more practical. A quick glance in the mirror confirmed what she'd been thinking. Perhaps the ponytail was actually making her look a little younger than her twenty-eight years. Her brown eyes sparkled in anticipation of whatever small adventure she might encounter in the beautiful park-like gardens. She was definitely ready for a stroll in the fresh air.

Holly knew, from the phone conversation she had with the senator that Seven Oaks wasn't just a home, but that a farm was part of the property as well. In addition, Drew VanDorn was part owner of several other businesses. This was probably the reason why he needed someone to assist him with his office work, particularly since he was still pretty much involved in politics as well.

At any rate, he'd been farsighted enough to provide for himself should he, some day, tire of the political arena. She had no idea -- hadn't really given it much thought, if there were any children, any heirs to all that the senator owned. All she had been told was that his wife had died many years ago. Considering this man's position in life, she was almost afraid at the thought that she might be a child of this man whom she had sought out for the purpose of answering that very question.

Wandering slowly through the grounds, she found herself on a path between neatly cut hedges that, occasionally, gave way to colorful flowerbeds. Some of these blooms were so exotic that the young woman could not have put a name to them; but since it didn't really matter what they were called, she feasted her eyes on them, enjoying the vibrant colors so much more after having been cooped up with her mother for such a long time.

Soon she was walking under stately old trees. This made Holly again consider the odd fact that the house had been given the name Seven Oaks when there was evidence of only the six that grew around the pond at the entrance.

Of course, there were many more such trees where she was now walking, but they weren't nearly as tall or stately and didn't appear as old, and certainly didn't do justice to the name of the manor.

At the end of the park the flowers, as well as the trees ended, and the small lane led Holly out of the shade and into the open where the sunshine lay warm on her back. She found herself walking between golden wheat fields stretching along both sides of the path. These fields must be part of the senator's property, Holly thought as she strolled slowly along the narrow road. The fields looked well cared for, but there wasn't a soul to be seen, and she enjoyed the solitude and the fact that she was able to hear the chirping of the birds hidden in some bushes that marked a bend in the road.

Coming around the curve, Holly couldn't help but smile when she glimpsed the figure of a man sitting with his back against a tree. He was wearing cut-off jeans, and his shirt was bunched up behind his head. Holly watched him as he kept gazing intently at the sky as though trying to penetrate its mysteries. He didn't notice her until she was standing next to him. That's when he lowered his head and, apparently became aware of her presence for the first time; however, he showed no surprise at seeing a strange young woman standing in front of him. He took his time before he said anything, looking her over from head to toe. He appeared to like what he saw.

Holly certainly felt that way about him. Her stomach did a little flip-flop when his eyes reached her face. He was quite good-looking, she thought. Having been deprived of male company for so long, she might have found any young man pleasing. But she was certain that this member of the opposite sex would have been regarded as a truly handsome specimen by most any female who came in contact with him. Somehow he made her feel very feminine, without ever having said a word. She hadn't even realized until this very moment, that she had missed this emotion very much.

Even though he was sitting down, she could tell he was tall. His hips were narrow, his shoulders broad. She judged his age to be between thirty and thirty-five. The bronze shade of his smooth skin indicated that he spent much of his time outdoors. A narrow face, a dark brown cap of wavy hair and deep blue eyes completed the picture.

"Hi, beautiful stranger," he greeted her at last, having given both of them time to look each other over. "Where to?"

"I don't know," Holly answered. "I just arrived at Seven Oaks today and decided to look around while I had the opportunity."

His eyes revealed a definite interest in Holly, and her heart skipped a beat, "Are you the senator's new secretary?" he wanted to know.

When Holly nodded yes, unable to speak through her jumbled up feelings, he jumped up and offered his hand.

"Then we'll be seeing a lot of each other," he informed her. "By the way, my name is Michael.

Holly had absolutely no objections to seeing this young man again. She quickly introduced herself as well, telling him only her first name, as he had done.

"Do you also work for the senator?" she wanted to know.

Michael grinned, "You might call it that. How about it," he changed the subject, "Will you keep me company for a little while longer?" He sat back down again and spread his shirt on the soft grass next to him, patting it invitingly.

Holly was beginning to relax a little. After all, Michael seemed to be a very nice young man, and why shouldn't she have feelings for him, even if things were moving a little fast for her. It did occur to her that she had been out of circulation much too long and had no idea how to proceed. Hopefully, it wouldn't take much to get her social life flowing again.

"You don't seem to take your work very seriously,"

she remarked, acting stern, but then she smiled and sat down to show she hadn't really meant it. There was something about this young man; a certain impression that seemed to pull her toward him; a feeling that she couldn't quite identify. And she sensed that he felt the same toward her.

Michael grinned again. "The senator might be strict," he said, "but he doesn't mind if his workers take a well-earned break now and then. Besides, I'm sure he understands that his new, very attractive secretary will turn the heads of all his male work force."

"That's a little too much flattery," Holly looked at Michael suspiciously. "And it sounds as though you've had some practice."

Michael shook his head and looked at her seriously, "It's not flattery," he assured her. "I mean every word of it. I like you, Holly, and I would love to get to know you better. Would you consider going to dinner with me before long?"

Holly's heart beat a little faster as her eyes locked with his and her stomach did that little flip-flop again. There was a glint in those dark blue eyes, a spark that echoed her own feelings, leaving her speechless once again, although for a brief moment only. But she was able to nod her consent.

When Michael moved a little closer and their bare arms touched accidentally, the sudden surge that went through her body was very similar to what she imagined an electric shock would feel like. It almost took her breath away. She rose quickly to her feet. Things were definitely moving too fast now. She hadn't dated in such a long time, really hadn't had any contact with men except for her mother's doctor. She had never felt this way before and was not certain how to handle it. Also, she felt slightly intimidated by Michael since he seemed to have such an easy way about him and she felt so stiff and, yes, naive.

"I have to go," she whispered breathlessly, not able to meet his eyes this time.

Michael's smile was a little uncertain. Had he guessed what was going on inside her? Holly wondered.

As if to make sure that she hadn't changed her mind, he repeated his earlier question, "But we will have that dinner, right?"

Again Holly nodded her head, "You know where I live. Call me."

Michael, at last, stood up, too. He placed his hand on his heart and looked at her candidly.

"I won't have to call you," he informed her. "My feelings tell me that I will see you again very soon."

Something was different. Holly noticed it on her way back to her new home.

Did the birds seem to be chirping more happily? Surely, the light breeze that lifted her short bangs was softer and milder... And wasn't she walking more light-footed than before? Even the sun seemed to be shining a little brighter.

The young woman stopped in her tracks when it suddenly occurred to her what had happened. She had fallen in love! Head over heels in love -- with a man she'd barely just met.

She, who had never before believed that love at first sight existed, was now experiencing the phenomenon herself. She still couldn't believe it, but that's all it could be.

She smiled at the very thought of it.

Chapter 5

As it turned out Holly was to see Michael a lot sooner than she had expected. After coming back from her walk, she managed to find her way back to her room without having to ask anybody's help, although she did make a few wrong turns along the way. It took her some time to decide what to wear for the evening meal. She'd forgotten to ask how formal her new employer expected his dinner guests to dress. After some deliberation, she settled for a white satin blouse and a long dark skirt that was brightened by the pale blue flowers printed on the lightweight fabric.

After unpacking and then laying out all of the things she planned to wear at dinner, she suddenly felt exhaustion overtake her. It had been a long morning and could possibly turn into a late evening. Not knowing what the family's habits were, Holly decided not to take any chances on possibly falling asleep while in her new employer's presence. It might not be a bad idea to lie down for a short nap, she decided.

A knock on her door woke her from a sound sleep. Gertrude was letting her know that it was time to go downstairs. She'd not forgotten that Holly was new at the manor and might not be able to find her way to the dining room, so she'd stopped by her suite to show her the way. While Holly quickly dressed, Gertrude waited for her in the living room. Holly was glad to find such a considerate person in Gertrude. She had a feeling that the two of them would get along beautifully.

Senator VanDorn was waiting for them in a small

room adjacent to the dining room. He was having a glass of wine; and he was not alone.

Holly's breath caught in her chest when she recognized Michael. Although she didn't realize it, it was impossible for the two men, and even Gertrude, not to notice the delight she apparently felt on seeing the young man. Her whole face lit up the minute she recognized him. He gave her a big, warm grin in return, pleased that his surprise had been such a success.

"Miss Snyder," the senator turned to her, "I would like to introduce you to my son, Michael."

Holly's smile disappeared from her face and was replaced by a bewildered look, mixed with near panic. Then her face turned pale. The sudden change in her demeanor did not escape Michael who had expected a very different reaction to his father's announcement. Surprise, perhaps, or pleasure -- but not this.

Gertrude had already seated herself next to the senator, who poured her a glass of the same red wine he was drinking. She hadn't failed to notice the strange exchange between the two young people, first Michael's happy grin on seeing Holly, then the senator's introduction of his son, which was followed almost immediately by Holly's apparent shock. Having no idea what to make of it, she kept her observations to herself.

Only the senator appeared oblivious to what had taken place just then.

Michael, however, was concerned about Holly's somewhat unexpected response. "I hope you aren't angry that I didn't confide in you earlier," he said, looking at her with those dark blue eyes. "I thought it might be fun to surprise you with the fact that we would be having dinner together so soon after I had invited you"

Holly shook her head and forced herself to smile, "No, of course I'm not angry," she answered as calmly as she could manage. "I'm simply a little stunned, as well as a little ashamed at my having talked in such a casual manner with the son of my employer."

The young woman's attempt to appear calm, now that she had digested the news to some extent seemed to be somewhat successful since Drew VanDorn still had not been able to detect any kind of change in her demeanor after having been introduced to his son. However, he seemed to have noticed that they were not total strangers.

"You two know each other?" He asked as he looked from one to the other of the young people, surprise written all over his face. He couldn't imagine where Michael and the new secretary might have met before.

Michael laughed, "Holly, that is, Miss Snyder," he corrected himself quickly, "caught me this afternoon while I was goofing off, and enjoying the wonderful weather we've been having lately. We'd never seen each other before then."

The senator laughed, "I hope she gave you a good talking to, about the fruits of labor and so on."

He glanced in Gertrude's direction, apparently wondering how dinner was progressing. The housekeeper put her wineglass on the small marble-topped table next to her. At about the same time an elderly woman, who Holly presumed to be the cook since she was wearing a long, white apron, had entered the room. The two women quietly exchanged a few words.

"Is it time to go in to dinner?" VanDorn inquired.

When Gertrude nodded her head, he rose and led the small group into the dining room next door.

"Not quite," Michael was answering his father's last question which the senator had directed at him, although the latter had almost forgotten what he'd asked. "In fact," Michael continued, "we visited for a little while and had a great time."

While he was talking, he didn't take his eyes off Holly. "But I have a feeling that she is angry with me now because I only gave her my first name and didn't tell her who I am," he now explained to his father.

Holly shook her head but, once again, was unable to look into Michael's eyes, only for a different reason, this time. How could she tell him the real reason why she was acting in this manner? It was all so complicated, and she would rather wait to say anything until she had some answers to the questions she'd come here to ask. She was feeling the beginnings of a headache, brought on by tension. Her temples were beginning to throb.

The small group seated themselves around the lavishly set dinner table, with the senator at the head and Gertrude next to him on one of the long sides of the table. Holly was directed to sit across from her, while Michael's place was next to Gertrude. Sitting almost across the table from Michael made it difficult for Holly to keep her eyes off him, although it was just as difficult, to look at him. So, she picked up her spoon and started to eat the soup, although she didn't feel the least bit hungry and, at any rate, could not have said what kind of soup it was.

"I think I'm just a little tired," she tried to explain the sudden change in her attitude toward the senator's son. "First I had that long drive, and now I have to digest all of the new impressions that I have experienced since my arrival."

While she was eating -- picking at the excellent food might have been a better way of putting it -- Holly barely looked up, but could feel Michael glancing in her direction every now and then. She could well understand why he would be puzzled by her change of behavior toward him. It was also evident that he had not bought her flimsy explanation.

While they were eating desert, strawberry shortcake, normally one of Holly's favorites, the senator asked her some personal questions she would rather not have had to answer just then. It was quite embarrassing to her to have him question her about her private life, when she was the one who had come here to do the same, only in reverse. However she did not yet feel comfortable enough to ask him what she was so determined to find out about his private life. She wanted to wait with that until after she got to know him a little better. So, when he asked about her mother's illness, she gave him only vague answers.

Immediately after the meal was over, Holly excused herself by mentioning her headache and started to hurry up the stairs toward her rooms. She was sure she would be able to find them now without assistance. However, Michael caught up with her before she had reached the first step.

"Please wait," he begged. He looked so confused and unsure of himself that Holly couldn't help but feel sorry for him. But, she still couldn't see herself even consider confiding in him. She simply couldn't let him know just yet what was bothering her. First, she had to work that out for herself. Perhaps after she had received the answers to her questions she'd come here to pose, she might be able to tell him her real reason for her abrupt attitude change. Right now she barely knew him and had no idea what his reaction would be if he knew about the thoughts that were going through her mind. She decided it would be much safer to keep her distance for the time being.

"Our date," he reminded her, "How about tomorrow evening?"

Holly hesitated, and then steeled herself to tell him what she thought was necessary at this point to keep him at bay for now. "I've changed my mind, "she therefore told him. "I've decided that it's not a good idea for us to see each other on a personal basis. Besides, according to what you said earlier, we've already had our dinner date tonight, I think that is sufficient for now."

"What has made you change your mind since this afternoon and what has made you become so prickly toward me?" he wanted to know, the disappointment noticeable in his voice. "I don't believe the only reason you no longer want to see me is the fact that you now know who I am. There has to be something besides that which is bothering you, something much more important." Suddenly his face lit up. "Are you afraid that my father would be opposed to our meeting privately because you work for him? Please believe me, he is not that old-fashioned. Your working for him would have no bearing on what you do in your private life."

"Oh, I believe you," Holly answered. "In spite of that I prefer not to accept your invitation." She wished he would leave her alone. She didn't know how much longer she would be able to stand his pleading without finally giving in. She realized that he had to be totally confused by her actions, but there was nothing she could do about that, at least not right now.

Michael started to say something else in an effort to convince her to change her mind, but she cut him off, "Please accept my decision," she said, trying to sound as firm as was possible under the circumstances. "And you can believe me when I say I am tired." With that she put an end to the conversation, by turning her back on him and quickly ascended the stairs.

She was relieved to be able to enter her bedroom at last. Here she no longer had to pretend. Taking a deep breath she closed the door and leaned against it for a moment with her eyes closed. She felt drained. How dreadful this day had ended after such a hopeful beginning. Michael's final pleadings had just about done her in. Her eyes filled with tears that squeezed through her lowered lids, and slowly trickled down her cheeks. She had to press her lips together to keep from sobbing out loud.

She remembered how happy she'd been just a few hours ago, and the pain of it just about doubled her over. Why did this have to happen? Why did she have to fall in love with the man who could very well be her half-brother? And how would she be able to handle living under the same roof with him day after day?

Chapter 6

Michael was visibly upset when he returned to the dining room. Gertrude Walters, who had stayed to join the senator for a final cup of coffee, now sensed that the two men might have something to discuss in private, so she decided to bid father and son a good night before discretely leaving for her own quarters.

Drew VanDorn looked at Michael with an indulgent smile on his face, "Am I correct in assuming that you like my new secretary?"

Michael shrugged his shoulders unhappily, "This afternoon I got the impression she liked me, too. This evening she suddenly does a complete turn-around. Perhaps I should have told her right away that I'm your son, although I'm not totally convinced that's the only reason she's been acting so strangely and has distanced herself from me ever since she found that out," he took a deep breath. "I just can't imagine what in the world made her have such a sudden and complete change of mind in her attitude toward me. She was so outgoing and friendly when she talked to me earlier. Tonight, after you introduced her, she would hardly look in my direction. Did you notice, also, that she barely ate anything? None of this makes any sense to me," Michael looked questioningly at his father. "I would have thought that the long trip from the city would have made her hungry. And I think she skipped lunch altogether, or so Gertrude indicated."

The senator took some time to respond to his son's remarks while slowly lighting one of his expensive cigars. With obvious enjoyment, he took a few puffs, blowing the blue-tinged smoke toward the high ceiling, before turning his attention back to Michael.

"You have made several points," he conceded, "but you probably didn't know that Miss Snyder has been spending an extensive amount of time with her ill mother. So you might consider that she is no longer used to being around other people. Perhaps she is intimidated by the fact that, due to her financial circumstances, she is suddenly forced to be in such close proximity to strangers." The senator exhaled another cloud of smoke.

Mike weighed the things his father had said in his mind, but dismissed them quickly. Holly hadn't seemed the type to be easily intimidated. It had appeared at their earlier meeting that she was not the least bit unsettled by him or their conversation. Something must have happened between then and the time they met again. The young man turned to his father.

"I don't think that was the reason. There has to be something else."

VanDorn leaned back in his chair and stared at the ceiling, "That leaves only one other possibility that I can see," he told Michael. "She doesn't want to be thought of as a fortune hunter like so many of your young lady friends who have generally been more after your money, and position in the community, and not so much after you. I think that actually speaks well for Holly," he added quietly.

Michael jumped up angrily, "That doesn't sound very flattering. A stranger might think you don't have a very high opinion of me either if you think that all of my former girl friends have only dated me because you have money."

"You know that's not true," the senator pointed out, "But as you know very well, there have been women in your life who were more interested in the material things you were able to offer them as I've already mentioned. If you really care for this young woman, you should be glad that this does not seem to be the case with her."

Michael considered again what his father had said.

Finally he shook his head and looked at his father, "Much as I hate to admit it, what you just said about the other women does seem to be true in most cases. But, even though I don't know Holly Snyder very well at this point, I'm convinced that she's not the kind of woman who cares much about community standings or money. And I'm just as certain that she'd be more likely to follow her heart, which she clearly indicated to me this morning. That's why I'm so puzzled and, yes, frustrated, by her attitude this evening. I just can't figure out what's gotten into her since this morning. I surely wish she would let me know what it is that is bothering her. But she is very secretive about whatever it is."

The young man looked at his father without really seeing him while he was trying to determine how he might get Holly to open up to him.

"Maybe I can get Gertrude to do a little investigating for me. Holly might possibly tell another woman what has set her against me since we first met this morning, and what has changed her mind about me so drastically."

"I wouldn't do that," Drew VanDorn told him. "I don't think it's a good idea to get Gertrude involved in this. You might place both of the ladies into an embarrassing situation. Just give it a little time," the senator added. "Things just might work out on their own."

"I still think there has to be another reason why she suddenly doesn't want to have anything to do with me," Michael wasn't able to let the matter rest just like that. "I can sense it, but I have no idea what it might be."

"As I already said, give her, as well as yourself, some time," the senator was starting to lose patience with his obstinate son. But he smiled when he added in a more soothing tone, "Your mother didn't make it easy for me either, at least not at first. In spite of that, we were very happy during our short marriage."

Michael could tell that his father's thoughts had

gone back to the past. He could see a shadow of pain crossing the older man's face. He knew what his mother had meant to his father, although he himself couldn't remember her at all. He'd been only a toddler when she had died.

"Haven't you ever considered marrying again?" he now asked quietly.

His father shook his head, "It would be too much to expect of any woman not only to have to live with me, but with my memories as well. If your mother had died differently I might not have had such a difficult time with it all, but as it is..." his voice trailed away.

Even so, Michael hoped that, some day, he would be able to love a woman as deeply as his father had loved his mother. Holly might just be that woman if she would allow him to come closer and find out what was troubling her. But he was not about to give up hope this soon. They had plenty of time to get better acquainted and smooth out whatever rough spots there were between them, whether they were real or just in Holly's imagination.

At age thirty-two, Michael was not at all inexperienced in matters concerning the opposite sex. Women had never made it difficult for him when it came to dates or getting to know them. But it was as his father had said, and as it had become all too clear to him as he got older and even more experienced, they all seemed to be after the senator's son and his money, not after the person that was Michael. On the other hand, he had never had any deep feelings for any of the women he'd dated -- not until today -- despite the fact that the two of them hadn't even had a date yet. Never had he been so much in love -- and after such a short time. He'd known instantly, as soon as he'd seen her: this is the one; this is the woman I want to spend the rest of my life with.

Michael hadn't noticed how closely his father had been watching him while he was sitting there, contemplating what might be his fate. Only when the senator addressed him, did he look up. "I had intended to ask you to check on our holdings in Texas; to have a look at the farm; to see how things are going down south." The senator had the feeling that this was not the right moment to ask this of his son, and he said so. "I don't suppose that you consider this to be a good time for you to leave here?"

Michael considered his father's request for a few minutes before giving his answer,

"Why not? It might not be a bad idea if I left for a little while to give us both time to think things over. Besides, Holly did ask me to respect her decision not to go out with me and I must admit, under the circumstances it will be difficult for me to ignore her if I have to see her day after day. And she might just feel sorry about the way she treated me if I disappear for a little while." He gave his father a lop-sided grin, not really believing what he had just said.

The senator, however, agreed with his son about him leaving for a short while. That's why he had mentioned the trip to Texas in the first place. A very reliable manager was in charge of the farm, although just to be on the safe side, he or Michael made an occasional appearance there. And the farm was as good a place as any to get away from it all, and it wouldn't hurt for Michael to gain some distance from his problem. His son must have truly fallen for this young lady, the senator mused. He had never seen him carry on this way before. Hopefully things would work out for both of the young people in the long run.

"So, when do you plan to leave?" he asked.

Michael decided that it would probably be best not to put it off. "I'll leave first thing in the morning," he told his father. Once he'd made up his mind to go, he didn't see any point in dragging out his departure. But, while a journey like the one he was about to undertake normally brought forth feelings of anticipation and excitement for the senator's son, this time he felt depressed, almost hopeless, something the usually optimistic young man didn't experience often. And the feeling that there was more to Holly's unexpected rebuff than she would admit to him persisted.

As Michael left the next morning, he had no idea how long he would be gone. He would play it by ear.

Chapter 7

Holly's new job presented no problems for her. Although she was, indeed, a little rusty, as she had told her new employer, doing office work was just like riding a bicycle -- once you knew how to do it, you never forgot. Also, this work was closely related to the job she'd held before her mother had fallen ill. So, it didn't take her long to get back in the swing of it, and it felt good that she was having no trouble taking care of the senator's office demands. She had always learned quickly and the papers that had literally covered her desk earlier were soon sorted and stacked in neat piles ready to be tackled by her in order of importance.

While the senator was quite satisfied with her work, he made it clear to her that she meant as much to him as a person as she did as a secretary, and treated her as a valued member of his household.

It had been two long weeks since Michael had left to oversee some of the work on the farm in Texas. At first Holly had felt guilty over his leaving, thinking he had done so to get away from her after the way she had treated him that first evening. But, she had since learned that he made these trips regularly, which led her to believe that he'd already had another one marked on his calendar and that it had been time, once again, to see how things were going in Texas. Whether it had been a coincidence that he had left that very next morning, she didn't know. She suspected that part of the reason for his sudden departure had been due to their confrontation. He had most likely left deliberately at that particular time to get away from her and to allow things to cool down between them.

What she didn't understand was how she could miss a person so terribly much, when she'd only known him for a few hours. The only thing that made any sense to her at all was that, much as she hated to think so, they must be brother and sister. Why else did she have this feeling of closeness, this feeling of belonging she'd had when she had been near Michael. She simply did not, and never would, believe in love at first sight. Yes, she had almost convinced herself, it had to be the blood they shared that made them feel so close to each other and she knew without a doubt that Michael felt the same way.

Once Michael had called to talk to his father and Holly had been the one to answer the phone. As soon as she heard his voice, her stomach did the now familiar flip-flop, and she could feel her heart beat clear into her throat. But she hadn't wanted him to notice how happy it made her to hear him speak, so she'd continued to keep her distance, even over the phone, and she'd kept her voice as cold as she was able. Her heart cried out to be with him, but she could never allow him to know the extent of her true feelings for him.

A few days later, Holly was typing some letters into her computer, when she heard a strange noise. Holding her fingers still, she listened. There it was again -- it sounded like someone was moaning as though in pain. And it was coming from the senator's office.

With the door between the two offices always open a crack, Holly was able to look into the other room after she rose from her chair. What she saw made her eyes open wide in horror. The senator was slumped sideways in his chair, his face distorted by, what must have been severe pain, his hand pressed over his heart. What was even more frightening to Holly was that the moaning seemed to have stopped.

Holly raced toward him, giving her shin a painful bump as she rushed around the corner of her desk. Drew VanDorn's face was the color of chalk. Small beads of perspiration stood on his forehead. He was unconscious.

The young woman, used to medical emergencies through her mother's long illness, reached for the phone and called the house number of the housekeeper. When Gertrude Walters answered, Holly told her as calmly as she was able under the circumstances that the senator seemed to have suffered a heart attack. Gertrude arrived only a few minutes later, having called both 911 and the senator's personal physician.

As worried as Holly was about her boss, it was nothing compared to the agonies Gertrude seemed to be suffering when seeing her employer in such a condition. It quickly became clear to Holly that the housekeeper felt much more for the senator than an employee normally would. Holly suspected that the woman loved the older man. Not wanting her to realize that she'd been found out, something Gertrude surely didn't want to happen after apparently having guarded her secret for all those years, Holly put her arms around the other woman. She knew how it felt when a loved one became ill. She suspected that she would feel the way Gertrude now did if anything should happen to Michael. And now Holly hoped she was telling the truth when she told the housekeeper that everything would be fine, but that she would have to hang in there for right now so that she could be there for the senator.

Those words seemed to be exactly what Gertrude needed to hear. Holly could actually feel the housekeeper standing taller as she straightened her spine and tried to pull herself together.

However, hard as she tried, Gertrude Walters didn't seem to be able to stop crying until the doctor, having examined his patient thoroughly, motioned the women into Holly's office.

Dr. Mark Ehmke appeared to be close to sixty years of age, about the same age as the senator, Holly guessed, but that's where all comparison ended. The senator was meticulous in his dress, always looking elegant, no matter what the occasion. Holly had never seen him in anything other than a suit and tie, while the doctor evidently preferred the casual look and was wearing jeans and a sweater along with jogging shoes. His salt and pepper hair was cut short, but he sported a small goatee that looked ludicrous in its bright red glory. Dr. Ehmke looked like a man who loved to laugh; however, at the moment the expression on his face was very serious. He appeared angry about something.

"That stubborn mule," he fumed, and then turned to the women, obviously somewhat embarrassed to have called the senator a name in front of them, particularly since the man he had been talking about in such a fashion happened to be quite sick. "Pardon me, ladies, for being so blunt," he apologized gruffly, "but I've told him again and again that he should take it easy." He looked at Gertrude, holding up his hand when he noticed she was about to interrupt, but apparently needing to get everything said first. "I warned him that his heart wouldn't take much strain -- that he was close to an incident. But would he listen to me, his good friend as well as doctor? Of course not. I hope this little episode has finally taught him a lesson, although I doubt it!"

"How is he?" Gertrude was only interested in her employer's condition. Right now she didn't want to hear about what had made him get sick. That could wait until later.

"At the moment, quite well," the doctor answered. "I gave him an injection." He noticed the EMTs who were waiting to see if they would be needed. "You can go," he told them. "This time it's not too bad -- but who knows about next time," he added under his breath. Then he turned to the women again. "A shot, of course, won't solve the problem. The senator needs to change his whole lifestyle. But instead, of listening to me, he insists on going back to work and calls me an old quack for warning him against it." Dr. Ehmke rubbed the bridge of his nose, and then looked angrily at the half-open door to the

A Mother's Sins

senator's office. No sound had, so far, come from the other room.

Gertrude Walters smiled through her tears, "He must be doing better if he's able to complain."

The doctor was, however, not so happy. "He was lucky this time," he explained. "It was only an angina attack. Next time it could be much worse, and to prevent that from happening, I want to be sure he doesn't return to his office for the rest of the week, and possibly even longer. We'll have to see how quickly he recovers his strength."

He looked at Gertrude, "I'm depending on you to keep an eye on this pigheaded fool, and make sure he follows my orders. Oh, and one other thing, I have also told him to skip the cigars. To be more accurate, I forbid them. Those things are poison for the man's heart."

Gertrude kept nodding her head to everything the doctor was telling her. "You can depend on me," she promised. "May I see him now?"

"Yes, but only for a minute. He needs to get to bed as soon as possible. And don't forget, no more cigars and, if at all possible, no excitement. As soon as you've seen him, you had better get somebody to help him to his room and into bed where he needs to stay for a while to get some rest."

"Yes, doctor, I will see to it that all of your orders are followed, "the housekeeper didn't linger and rushed into the senator's office. Holly thought it best to let Gertrude see the senator by herself so didn't try to go into the other office. Instead she walked with the doctor who had, up to that time, been too busy to pay any attention to her. Although he seemed to know his way around, she accompanied him down the stairs and to the entry doors. The doctor was apparently still deep in thought, probably trying to decide how best to make his stubborn patient take better care of himself. Near the door he suddenly gave her a sidelong glance and exclaimed, "Hello there, I don't believe I've seen you here before. Who might you be?"

"Holly Snyder," Holly introduced herself. "Senator

VanDorn's new secretary. You see, he wasn't totally ignoring your orders. He did hire me to help him with his work"

The doctor looked at her, but his mind was evidently still with the difficult patient he'd left upstairs and, even though Holly was standing right next to him he, again, didn't seem conscious of her presence. She wasn't even sure he'd heard what she'd said just now. His demeanor was tense. But suddenly his face lit up, making him seem a totally different person. He gave her a big smile. Her words must have finally hit home.

"Did I hear you say you're Drew's new secretary? In that case, you're just what the doctor ordered, excuse the pun. Not only can you help take some of the workload off your new boss, but you can also help Gertrude make sure he follows my orders since you will be around him to keep an eye on the man. Miss Snyder, you couldn't have come at a better time."

With that he turned and had disappeared through the front door before Holly had a chance to respond to his words.

A Mother's Sins

Chapter 8

"I'm sorry," said Able Smith, president of Second State Bank, after looking at the documents spread out on his desk. "You've used up all of your credit with us. We're no longer able to let you borrow any money."

Margaret O'Mally shook her head from side to side, causing her mane of bright red hair to appear as though flickering flames were surrounding her face as the curls flowed in all directions. This can't be, she thought, this just can't be! But she wasn't going to give that stupid banker the satisfaction of seeing her worried. Instead she looked down her almost aristocratic nose at the man seated across the desk from her, a man whom she had known for many years, and who, at this moment in time, could possibly be holding her destiny in his hands.

"What do you mean, you're not able to loan me more money?" She asked, pretending ignorance. "I've gotten money from you a number of times in the past without any problems. What's different this time? Am I no longer the Margaret O'Mally who inherited her parents' ranch along with their money?" She looked at the banker, fury sparkling in her green eyes. "I would not have traveled all the way from Monte Carlo to Dallas, had I known I would receive a negative answer to my need of money." The young woman almost spit the last words at the banker.

The man's face remained impassive. He'd dealt with this sort of problem a number of times in the past. In fact, he'd seen Margaret in action before, although her anger had not been directed at him that time. "I'm sorry I can't give you better news, Miss O'Mally," he said in a voice that didn't in any way indicate that he was truly sorry. "However, this information couldn't and shouldn't have been that unexpected on your part. After all, we've asked you repeatedly, by mail and by phone, leaving messages each time, for you to get in touch with us. Actually, in retrospect, we've bent over backward to keep you informed about your financial situation. There is nothing we can do if you don't pay attention to us."

"Well, I'm here now," Margaret answered, her irritation at the inconvenience obvious. "But all you tell me is that you can't loan me any more money." Abel Smith could have told her that her appearance at this late date, after numerous attempts had been made to notify her for several weeks, all of them ignored by the young woman, was much too late to do her any good. The messages that had been left, letting her know that if one borrowed money, one had to make an attempt to make the payments, seemed to have made no impression on her at all. And so he decided it would serve no useful purpose to upset the haughty Miss O'Mally any more than she already was by reminding her once more of this fact, and held his tongue.

However, Margaret was not finished with him, "Don't you have a boss I can talk to?" she asked. "Someone who will realize how wrong you are and will help me get the money I need?"

"Miss O'Mally," Smith was beginning to lose his patience with the headstrong young woman. "I am the president of this bank. Who do you suggest might be my boss?"

Margaret shrugged her shoulders. Such small details did not interest her. All she was looking for were results -- results in her favor.

The ranch that belonged to the beautiful young woman, who claimed that her early ancestors had been Irish royalty, although no one had ever seen this claim proven in any visible form, had been hopelessly neglected. Margaret was deeply in debt. She had spent and spent, throwing out money with both hands until there was nothing left.

At this point, Smith was only concerned with minimizing the losses the bank would sustain. He already knew that he would not be able to collect all of the money owed the bank by this woman. Had there been the smallest glimmer of hope that Margaret would use any money that came her way to build up the ranch and make it once more into the successful business it had once been, Smith might even have considered helping her one more time, if only to recoup his losses. But there wasn't the slightest chance of that ever happening. Margaret liked to spend money for only one reason, to indulge herself.

"I would like to hear how you plan to pay off your outstanding debts to us," he asked now without a hint of pity, deciding a frontal attack might be in order at this point.

Margaret gritted her teeth angrily. At the same time she felt panic rise within her. She was slowly beginning to realize that, while she had been living in luxury, her money had been melting away like an ice-cream cone on a summer day in Dallas. And she had enjoyed her expensive lifestyle without giving a thought to tomorrow and what she would do when the money was gone. She had taken the wealth with which she'd grown up for granted without considering that in order to have money to spend; it had to be earned first.

After her parents had died in that awful car crash, Margaret had initially drowned her sorrows in alcohol, and through her drinking sprees, she had become acquainted with members of the jet set and had, eventually, become a member herself. They had accepted her with open arms and had not hesitated to help spend her money. She had traveled the world and had never considered the cost of her lavish lifestyle. She lived like there was no tomorrow, giving no thought to how much money she was spending and that there might be an end to it some day. She stayed in expensive hotels, bought Parisian gowns that she wore once, then throwing them away or giving them to others who were a little more reluctant in spending their own money. She gave, what she considered, aristocratic parties to match her supposedly blue blood, and invited anyone with a name, good or bad.

The ranch, located near Houston, and left to her suddenly due the death of her parents, was left in charge of a foreman who'd been taking care of the O'Mally place for years. He had tried to do his best for Margaret, but his hands were tied because there was no money available to him for either repairs, or any kind of improvements. Much of the machinery and many of the tools were old and outdated and needed to be replaced. Again, there were no funds for such expenses. The man, at last, felt he had to say something to his young boss about economizing and that she would have to stop her spending if she wanted to save the ranch.

Margaret had been so furious at his audacity -- at the fact that this lowly person dared tell her, the heiress, the aristocrat, what to do, that she left the hotel in Monaco where his call had finally caught up with her, and returned home on the first flight she had been able to book. She did this for the sole reason of having the satisfaction of seeing his face when she fired him. She accused the poor man of being incapable of running a ranch and that she would see to things herself from now on. He left without much protest, although Margaret owed him several months back pay. She then proceeded to attempt the job herself, despite the fact that she was totally ignorant of running any kind of business.

Things at the ranch went downhill fast. Besides not having the faintest notion of what she was doing, she was also quickly bored with the simple life in the country. At any rate, she felt that the job was beneath her. Her father had always had a foreman to do the dirty work for him. It wasn't her fault that the one she'd fired had been lazy and no good. She didn't give it a thought that this was one and the same man.

But since, in her opinion, she shouldn't have to do

this kind of work, and since she couldn't find a decent person who would do the job for next to nothing, the work simply didn't get done at all.

And now her banker had turned against her, too.
She looked at the man sitting across from her, still waiting for an answer to his question, and she got an idea she thought was brilliant and would enable her to get rid of the whole mess.
"I will sell the ranch," she informed the bank president.
Smith didn't seem to be overly impressed by this bright, well-thought-out plan she thought she had just come up with.
"And who do you think will be interested in buying your property?" he asked. "As run down as it is right now, it will take a small fortune to turn it into a profitable business again, and most businessmen are interested in making money, not spending it." Not at all like a certain person I know, he thought to himself.
"Do you have a better idea?" the young woman spit out angrily.
"As I explained earlier, it's not up to me. You're the one with the debts, owing the bank -- and who knows how many others -- money, so I'm waiting for ideas from you," he answered sharply. "Ideas that will work and will help repay the money that you owe us. I don't suppose I have to remind you that your accounts have been frozen and, basically, you no longer have any money to spend. You can thank the fact that this bank had a long and satisfactory business relationship with your father and that, solely based on that fact; we've been lenient with you for this length of time. But there is a limit to what we can do for you, and, I'm afraid, that limit has now been reached. This is the end of our business relationship. The only thing we are interested in now is for you to repay your loan."
Margaret jumped up, her red hair flying around her

head like bright tongues of fire.

"I don't think I have to tolerate your insults," she shouted, heading toward the door.

Abel Smith also stood up. "I'm sorry that our conversation had to take this turn," he said, sounding somewhat milder now. "I do, however, want to make it clear that something will have to be done immediately about reducing your debts with us. Otherwise the remainder of your former wealth will be lost and you might end up without a roof over your head. And if worse comes to worse, we might decide to take you to court. I'd hate to see that pretty hair of yours get cut off while you're in prison, although I might be very tempted to do something along those lines myself if I don't see you at least make an attempt to live within whatever means you have left to you and pay back what you owe."

Smith knew it would serve no purpose to sue Margaret since she had nothing left worth suing for, but he thought the idea of prison might frighten her enough to do some soul-searching; to do some serious thinking about the situation in which she found herself.

His last words did frighten the young woman. But she was not about to let him know this. And she was not willing to continue the conversation with the president of the bank since he did not intend to help her anyway. He seemed only intent to insult her, and she did not have to take that from anyone. Without another word, she turned on her heel and headed, once more, toward the door. Before she could reach it, Smith called her back one more time.

"I just remembered something that might be helpful to you. Michael VanDorn, the son of Senator VanDorn, happens to be visiting his family's farm just now, the one that borders onto your property. You should talk to him. He's the one person who might possibly be interested in buying your ranch."

Margaret nodded to the man with all the arrogance she could muster and walked out of his office -- this time for good. Once outside, she stopped for a moment, taking several deep breaths. She would never have admitted this to anyone, but the unpleasant conversation she had just endured had taken its toll. It was difficult to walk in her high heels, while her knees where shaking as much as they were.

Right now, she felt as though there wasn't a living soul in the world who cared about her and her troubles. She was broke, and if a miracle didn't happen, she might lose her home. 'It would be awful if my friends should find out about all of this,' she thought unhappily. Without money, she knew, she would no longer be considered part of the jet set, and her former friends would drop her in a flash.

Ursula Turner

Chapter 9

"I don't care how important those papers are," Gertrude Walters said showing a side of herself Holly had not seen before. The woman was upset and worried, but there was anger in her words as well. "Surely you don't plan to go down to the archives, or...?" She didn't complete the sentence.

"Or?" The senator seemed to be in a rebellious mood. A good sign, Holly thought that he was feeling better at least, but she did agree with the housekeeper in that he surely wasn't well enough to descend the flight of stairs to the basement.

When Gertrude realized that she wasn't having any success in getting her boss to be reasonable while she put on her act of being angry with him, although it wasn't altogether an act, she decided to try the sly approach. "If you don't stay in bed, I will call Dr. Ehmke immediately," she warned.

"Please," VanDorn begged, "not that!" He fell back into his pillows. Actually he was glad that Gertrude had stopped him from going to the archives even if he would never let his housekeeper know it. He still felt weak. His recent attack had affected him more than he would have believed possible. At the same time, however, he felt guilty for what he considered wasting time. He wasn't used to spending time in bed during the day while mountains of work awaited his attention. Since he was hurting only a little, he didn't want to admit, even to himself, how serious his health problem might still become.

"I could get those papers for you," Holly offered, seeing how anxious both Gertrude and the senator were, even if for different reasons. "I do know my way around the manor pretty well by now and should be able to find the archives. Just point me in the right direction."

Since the senator had been ill, there hadn't been a lot for her to do, and she was, frankly, beginning to feel a little bored. While at her mother's bedside, she'd done some needlework, mostly embroidery, but expecting to be either busy with work or exploring her new surroundings, she hadn't brought anything like that along to keep her occupied. And the senator's taste in books didn't run along her lines of interest. So she was happy to be able to offer her services and find the papers her boss felt he needed so urgently.

The senator sat up again, new hope in his eyes. "Would you really do that for me? Then I could work on the contracts today and perhaps even finish them."

Holly smiled and shook her head glancing in the direction of the housekeeper, "Mrs. Walters would tear my head off," she said with another sideways look at Gertrude, "If my offer should cause you to do any kind of work. I will do the work on the contracts and you can check them and make whatever changes you feel are necessary."

The senator grinned, "I'll have to pat myself on the back. It was very smart of me to hire you," he said.

"I have to agree with you," Gertrude commented. "But now you need to rest, she ordered. "For the next hour I don't want to hear a sound coming from this room except maybe your snoring."

"It's time for Michael to come home," the senator complained. "I'm surrounded by bossy females and I don't think I can take much more of this." However, in truth he wasn't at all upset, but rather felt like he was being pampered more than he deserved. As ordered, he closed his eyes and was asleep by the time Holly and Gertrude had left the room, closing the door quietly behind them.

"Does Michael know his father is sick?" Holly asked the housekeeper.

"I called him," Gertrude nodded affirmatively, "and

after he heard the news he was going to drive back here immediately. I had all I could do to keep him from rushing home. I assured him that it would be in his father's interest that he, Michael, stay in Texas until his business there was finished. Otherwise, the senator would only have something else to worry about. But I had to promise Michael that I would call him immediately should his father's condition worsen. I don't think we will have to worry about that for the time being, though. He seems to be getting better. If we can only keep him down a little while longer." The housekeeper took a deep breath after her long speech.

"I will do my best to handle as much of his work as I can," Holly promised. "I hope that will keep him out of his office for now."

Gertrude impulsively hugged the young woman. "I'm so glad you're here," she said.

The cellars of the manor were just as confusing as the upper floors except that they were darker. Evidently each had been added on just as the main building had received its additions. Holly found the archives in what had been the original cellar. This room was neither dark nor musty, like the rest of the basement. Bright lights had been installed in the high vaulted ceiling at regular intervals, making the cavernous room as bright as daylight after Holly flipped the switch. She would have no trouble finding the documents she needed for the contracts.

She soon discovered that the archives not only held business-related papers, but also old folders that contained papers concerning the senator's family tree. In addition, Holly found a number of other personal documents. This was one of the reasons why the room had been equipped with air-conditioning. It kept the air dry and at a constant temperature to preserve all the older as well as the newer documents contained in the file drawers. It was so cool, in fact, that, despite the beautiful summer day outside Holly was glad she brought her cardigan after she'd been advised by Gertrude to do so. It had been difficult for her to imagine it being this cold anywhere with all that sunshine outside. Gertrude had finally convinced her that she would need something to keep from being chilled.

The more recent documents were kept in huge cabinets, and Holly quickly noticed they were sorted by dates, as well as in alphabetical order, with the year on the outside of each cabinet door. It didn't take her long to find the papers she'd come down here for. Folder in hand, she took a walk along the rows of filing cabinets -- farther and farther into the huge room -- until she spotted it -- a cabinet that was marked with the year of her birth.

Laying the folder down Holly slid the door to the cabinet open. She felt a little uncomfortable to be snooping through papers that were basically none of her business. Her feelings bordered on guilt when she considered how kind the senator had been to her, and she almost turned to go back upstairs. But then, hesitating for another moment, she asked herself, wasn't this the reason she had come here in the first place, to find out who she was and whether her new boss was also her father?

Her heart began to beat faster when she saw her mother's name. The senator had sent the money to her mother personally, she discovered. And Holly also found a letter from her mother in which she formally thanked him for his assistance. Wasn't that proof enough that what she had suspected was true?

Deep in thought, Holly pushed the door to the cabinet shut. Although she had no definite evidence, she no longer had any doubt about who her birth father was. Of course there was one sure way to obtain actual proof, one way she could be certain to find out what she wanted to know. She would simply have to find the courage to talk to the only person who was able answer her questions -- the one person who knew the truth.

She realized, of course, that this was not the right time to approach Drew VanDorn and ask him about her past and what he might be willing to tell her about it.

After all this time he might not want to discuss it at all, might even prefer not to admit that he had a daughter. She had no idea how he would react to the possibility that Holly might be this daughter. But the one thing that was more important to her than anything, even if she never found out about her past, was the senator's health. She did not want to take any chances on getting this kindly man excited to such an extent that it would cause him to suffer a second, more serious heart attack. Holly was in no way willing to take that chance. She would wait until her employer felt better.

She had come to like the man very much, and she knew his feelings for her were the same. She could wait a while longer to find out about her origins. Difficult as it was for her to put it off; she would ask her questions at a later time.

When Holly came back upstairs, she knocked on Senator VanDorn's door and, after receiving permission, entered, folder in hand. She was surprised to find a stranger sitting on a chair next to the senator's bed.

"Richard Storm, meet Holly Snyder, my almost new secretary and right hand," VanDorn introduced the two and, by way of an explanation, "Richard is my attorney. I asked him to stop by so I could make a couple of minor changes in my will. That little bout with my heart started me thinking..." He seemed reluctant to finish the sentence. Holly and the lawyer shook hands, after which she prepared to leave, assuming the men had business to discuss and didn't need her to hang around.

"No need to go, Holly," the senator said. "We've finished the formalities and were just talking about old times when you came in. Richard and Michael attended school together and we like to reminisce, that is, I do, while Richard probably just tolerates an old man's trip down memory lane." He waved off the attorney's protests. Holly sat on the edge of a chair. She listened absentmindedly while the two men continued to talk. Her attention kept straying from what they were saying as she examined

Richard Storm from under lowered lids. He evidently was about the same age as Michael. About thirty-two, she guessed. The elegant suit and silk tie he wore somehow made him look like a young boy playing dress-up. Holly could picture his muscular figure better in jeans and a t-shirt. His face looked as though he had shaved especially for the occasion of this visit. It was pretty much unlined as though he'd not suffered much stress during his life, but small creases at the corners of his eyes and mouth indicated that he liked to laugh, and did so often. His short hair was dark brown, as were his eyes.

When Senator VanDorn addressed her, Holly jumped. She'd been so intent on studying the visitor; she hadn't noticed that the men had finished their conversation and that the attorney was ready to leave.

"Did you hear me, Holly?" She finally realized that the senator was talking to her. When he saw he had her attention, he continued. "Would you mind showing Richard out? He has absolutely no sense of direction and gets lost every time he's here. In addition, I don't believe he's ever been to this part of the house, and would definitely not find his way out. We usually take care of business in my office, of course."

Holly smiled and walked to the door, the young attorney following her. Once in the hallway, Richard Storm placed his hand on Holly's arm to get her attention. She stopped and turned toward him.

"Would you go to dinner with me tomorrow?" he asked.

Holly looked at him in astonishment, "Do you always move this fast?" she wanted to know.

The young lawyer grinned. "What else can I do? I don't think I want to wait until the senator decides to change his will once more before I'll get a chance to come here and see you again."

The explanation was so ridiculous that Holly couldn't help but laugh. He seemed to be a very nice young man. She probably wouldn' t have hesitated for evena moment to accept his invitation if she weren't constantly thinking of one man. She had to get Michael out of her mind. She simply had to do something about that.

"I accept your invitation," she told Richard Storm, her voice firm. "Just let me know when."

Ursula Turner

Chapter 10

"You look wonderful." Richard Storm couldn't keep his eyes off the young woman as she slowly came down the last few steps of the curved staircase.

Holly was wearing an ankle-length, full-skirted white dress sprinkled with tiny blue flowers that brought out the blue in her eyes. She'd pinned up her hair, with just a few wispy tendrils framing her face, causing those expressive eyes of hers to be even more noticeable.

Before the two young people left the house, Richard insisted that they stop by the senator's room to see how he was doing. The doctor had been there earlier and Holly knew that the visit had left her employer quite grumpy. Much as she liked her boss, today she would not have minded to keep her distance. VanDorn, who had hoped to get up and go back to his work, had been told instead that he was still not allowed out of bed except for a couple of hours before lunch each day. And after the meal, he was to take a nap. The orders had not been received well, since VanDorn was feeling much better and saw no sense wasting more time in his bed. However, against her better judgment, Holly decided to join Richard on this visit, hoping that she might be able to cheer her employer up a bit.

To her surprise, the senator was in a much better frame of mind than when she'd seen him earlier.

"I hope you two have a great evening," he said, looking at Holly, "But don't let this guy fast-talk you into anything. You know how lawyers are. They have a silver tongue." He turned to Richard, "I'm glad to have found such a competent and efficient secretary," he continued, "and I would hate to have to do without her anytime soon."

Holly blushed at what she presumed the senator was implying, no, what he was actually insinuating, she amended the thought. She was a little angry at him for saying what he had, and wanted to tell him that she was only going out to dinner with this young lawyer, not to get married. But, since Richard Storm seemed to be ignoring the other man's words, she thought it best to do the same.

However, Drew VanDorn's thoughts had been with Michael who would probably not like the idea of Holly going on a date with the attorney. Of course, he could hardly tell Holly whom she could date. After all, she had made no secret of the fact, had actually made it fairly clear that she was not interested in his son. But he could still hope that she would change her mind about how she felt about Michael.

Holly had to admit that, after her initial reluctance to accept the young lawyer's dinner invitation she was actually enjoying her evening out. Richard took her to a restaurant that was located along the riverfront. Since it was a warm evening they sat outside on the deck. Their small table was covered with a red and white checkered cloth. A candle was flickering its small flame in the center, throwing mysterious shadows over their faces. Colored lanterns had been strung along the edges of the deck, enhancing the evening and casting a romantic atmosphere around the young couple. Holly looked dreamily at the water where not only the lanterns, but also a big yellow moon, were reflected on the lightly rippling surface.

"It's beautiful here," she told Richard.

"You're the one that's beautiful here, everything else pales in comparison," Richard couldn't keep his eyes of his young companion.

Once again Holly was blushing, thinking that her dinner companion was laying it on a bit thick. She was glad that the shadows and the flickering candlelight hid her flaming face. Having been cut off from the world for so long, she was not used to receiving compliments of any

A Mother's Sins

kind. "If you don't stop staring at me, or saying things like that, I'll get up and leave," she finally managed to get out and was only half joking as she said the words.

Richard looked around him and spread out his arms, "Every man here is looking at you. Haven't you noticed?"

Holly couldn't help herself and burst out laughing. She decided not to take Richard seriously. She felt secure in the young lawyer's company. When she thought about it, she decided that his compliments didn't embarrass her nearly as much as Michael's might have. But then, Michael was the man she loved. Despite everything she now knew, she still loved the senator's son so much that her heart hurt every time she thought about him. The knowledge that it was a forbidden love made it all the more unbearable. So it appeared almost like the hand of fate that she should have met Richard to help her forget the pain, even if only for a little while.

"A penny for your thoughts." Richard surely must have noticed that her mind wasn't on him, but he didn't indicate it in any way. However, it seemed that, if she wanted to get away from her heartache, he unquestionably was the man to help her, even if inadvertently. He was so easy-going and fun loving. Not at all the way Holly had imagined an attorney would act. But then, they were people like everyone else.

She smiled at his remark. "They're not worth even that much," she told him, reaching for the menu, which the waitress was just then handing her. Pretending to study it thoroughly gave her a chance to hide her face behind the pages to compose herself. She was still having minor problems being out with a man -- any man.

Richard Storm continued to make it easy for his pretty date to enjoy herself. All through the meal he entertained her with stories about some of the clients he'd had to deal with throughout his law career. Some of the tales were funny or crazy, while others were out-and-out scary. He actually admitted as much.

"These days I no longer deal much in criminal law," he told Holly. "I try to stick with corporate law. But once in a while a really interesting case comes along and I just can't turn it down. I have to test myself to see if I've still got it."

After dinner he suggested they go dancing. It seemed like forever since Holly had had an opportunity to do that. While she was taking care of her mother, there had been no time or even occasion for such pleasures. Now she wondered if she would remember any of the steps. However, since Richard was an excellent dancer it didn't take her long before she'd caught on to the rhythm again.

Having allowed the fast beat of the band to carry them along, they unexpectedly had to change their rhythm to the smooth, slow sounds of a love song. Richard held Holly close to him while she placed her arms around his neck and laid her head against his shoulder, closing her eyes. While Richard was guiding her across the dance floor, she saw, in her mind's eye, Michael holding her in his arms instead, until she could actually hear the loving words he was whispering in her ear.

Her bubble burst as soon as the music stopped. She opened her eyes and tilted her head back, looking straight up into Richard's friendly face instead of that of Michael, as real as that had seemed. Judging by the young man's longing expression, he was now in the bubble from which she herself had so abruptly been forced to emerge.

My God, thought Holly horrified, what am I doing? She had played with Richard's feelings, almost leading him on, without realizing it and he was, evidently, falling in love with her. Oh, how simple it would be if she could return his feelings, she thought, but she knew that would never happen.

"I think it might be a good idea for you to take me home now," she said softly.

Richard's disappointment was obvious, "The evening has just started," he objected.

"I actually think the new day is already beginning,"

was Holly's dry retort.

When the young man realized that he could not change Holly's mind, he gave in without further argument and reluctantly drove her home. After his car had come to a stop in front of the manor house, he turned off the engine as well as the lights before facing Holly.

"I don't suppose it would be a good idea if I tried to kiss you?" he asked, apparently sensing that her feelings for him were only those of a friend and that she did not feel the love for him that he hoped for.

Holly shook her head and smiled a little sadly, "No, not a very good idea," she agreed. She would have liked to touch him -- to run her hand through his thick, curly hair and along his cheek, simply to show him that she did like him. But in the end she was afraid he might misunderstand such a gesture, and she did not want to give him any more false hopes.

When he started to get out of the car to open her door, she stopped him and opened it herself.

"Thanks for a wonderful evening," she whispered as she got out of the car.

Richard waited until she had unlocked the big door and had stepped inside the manor before he drove off.

Ursula Turner

Chapter 11

"It was good of you to come." Gertrude Walters opened the door wide to allow the unexpected visitor to enter. She'd been trying to reach this man, the senator's closest friend, for several days now to let him know about VanDorn's health problems and consequent collapse, but he'd been out of the country on business. She'd finally decided it might be best if she let someone at his office know what had been happening so they could give him the news as soon as he returned. She'd been reluctant to leave a message on his answering machine, so as not to frighten the man unnecessarily.

"It's getting more and more difficult to keep him down," she complained to the visitor, after he'd stepped into the hallway. This man was someone she had known for a long time and she treated him as such. "Perhaps you can keep him occupied for a while, keep his mind off himself and the state of his health -- anything to make him stay put a while longer. It certainly wouldn't hurt if you could cheer him up a little."

Willard Graham could hear the smallest touch of relief in the housekeeper's voice. But she wasn't done yet. "The better he gets, the less he listens to me," she complained. "He wants to jump right back into work when he should be taking it easy for a few more days; actually for good if I had anything to say about it."

Graham laughed, "My dear Mrs. Walters, I believe you when you say he's not making things easy for you. I've known Drew for a many years and he never was one to sit still for any length of time. However, doesn't it seem like a good sign to you that he wants to be up and doing? I would think that the more he grumbles, the better he is actually feeling. Don't you agree?"

"Maybe you're right, "she conceded, "but he's always angry with me these days because I insist that he should follow the doctor's orders. It's just that I've never known him to act that way toward me."

Graham had long suspected how the housekeeper felt about the senator, but had kept his thoughts to himself. Much as he would have liked to see the two get closer to each other, he knew Drew, and knew also that he had never gotten over his wife's untimely death; that the man actually blamed himself for the way she had died. Graham felt that none of it was any of his business, and had decided a long time ago to keep his nose out of it. They were friends, yes, but they did not interfere in each other's lives.

Now he laughed out loud when he noticed Gertrude's pathetic expression, "I know my old friend well. I'm very familiar with his temperament, although I suspect he doesn't really mean it. It's like the old saying 'his bark is worse than his bite', or something like that. He would never intentionally mistreat anyone don't you know? He just can't stand it when he's forced to sit still." Graham shook his head, feeling a little sorry for his old friend and the problems he seemed to be facing. "I suppose right now he's acting downright impossible. How long has it been since this angina attack?"

"Let me think." The woman stopped as though that would help her remember better, although she knew exactly when the senator had fallen ill. "It's been a little more than a week now, but you'd think, by the way he acts, that he's had to stay down for months."

Gertrude had followed the visitor to the parlor while they'd been talking. There was no need to show him the way. He'd been to the manor many times before and knew where he would find his friend. He was certain that Drew would not be lingering in bed any longer, so the parlor had to be the place.

Graham did not enter the room immediately. Instead, he stopped for an instant in the doorway, seemingly somewhat taken aback by the sight of a young woman rising from her chair which had been placed along one wall and which he had to pass on his way to see the senator. He was sure he'd never met the young lady before, but yet, she looked oddly familiar to him. Graham couldn't seem to stop himself from staring at her.

Holly, in the meantime, thought that the stranger looked eerily familiar, although she couldn't recall actually having seen him before. He probably looks like someone I've known in the past, she told herself.

The senator, who for several days now had refused to remain in his bed, was instead reclining on a low sofa where he felt he wasn't quite as isolated from everybody and everything as he was in his room. At the sound of a man's heavy footsteps, he sat up and looked expectantly in the direction of the door. These days the smallest interruption broke up the boredom he was feeling so profoundly since he'd become ill. His face lit up when he saw Graham.

"My dear friend," he said, leaning forward and offering his hand. "How nice of you to come for a visit. It's about time you showed your face around here, though. I was beginning to think you didn't care whether I lived or died."

Graham hurried toward VanDorn, taking his outstretched hand in both of his. He took care not to show the shock he felt upon seeing his old friend's gaunt face. Drew's condition must have been much worse than he'd been led to believe. And the housekeeper had actually said the patient was doing better."

"You rascal," Graham tried not to let his voice show the concern he felt. "I can't believe that you would pull this kind of a stunt." He looked at VanDorn forcing a smile, "I think you just wanted some extra attention. But I do hope you'll be up and around again before too long. Of course you will. I don't believe that anything will keep you down for long. And I'm aching to get revenge for that last game of golf I lost to you."

"I would be up and working right now if certain people would let me," the senator grumbled, giving Gertrude, who was hovering anxiously in the background, a sideways glance.

Graham grinned and winked at the housekeeper. "I suggest that you are the one who's tyrannizing people, and then you get mad at them when they worry about your health, and try to take care of you. Shame on you!"

"Now you're turning against me, too," the senator protested.

"Instead of scolding everybody and feeling sorry for yourself, why don't you introduce me to this young lady?" Graham admonished his friend mildly, giving Holly a quick smile.

"That's right; you haven't met my new secretary, have you?" VanDorn did look the slightest bit guilty for thinking only of himself and his problems instead of remembering his good manners and introducing the two. "Holly Snyder, a very efficient young woman who has come to make my life easier -- Willard Graham, my very best friend -- at least so I thought until a few minutes ago."

Holly and Graham couldn't help but laugh at the senator's wry remark. They shook hands, each with a firm grip. Feeling the older man's touch caused an odd yet comfortable feeling to surge through Holly. She didn't understand why she should feel so safe in this man's presence. She didn't quite know what to make of this reaction to a total stranger, although she did know she could trust him since he was the senator's long-time friend. But the entire incident left her quite confused.

"Do we know each other?" With that question Graham admitted to similar feelings.

Holly shook her head, "I was thinking the same thing at first, but I'm sure we've never met."

"Strange." Graham couldn't keep his eyes off Holly. There was something about her... He was sorry when she excused herself and left the room. There seemed to be a big void after the door had closed behind her.

"An interesting young lady," he remarked to no one in particular. The senator didn't appear to have noticed anything unusual taking place between his friend and his employee, but he had heard Graham's remark, and wondered what he meant by it.

"What do you know about her?" Graham now wanted to know.

VanDorn grinned, "Don't you think she's a little young for you?"

Graham laughed in return, "You old fool. You, of all people should know that I have no interest in courting your secretary or any other woman. I'm just wondering why she looks so familiar to me. I keep thinking I've met her before.

"I really don't know that much about her." The senator was trying to think. "Both of her parents are dead, her mother having died more recently. I hired her because of her excellent papers as well as her outstanding references. She's quite efficient, thorough, and conscientious and, as I'm sure you've noticed, pretty as well. And as far as I know, she's not from around here. That's about all I can tell you. Now, let's play a game of backgammon. We haven't done that for a long time with both of us always so busy."

Graham was happy to oblige his friend. Gertrude had asked him to keep the senator occupied for a while and to distract him a bit. Let the poor man forget about his troubles for a couple of hours and get his mind on some more pleasant things.

But the visitor couldn't keep his mind on the game and wasn't even upset when he kept losing. VanDorn finally had enough. After he'd won his fifth game, he realized that his friend's thoughts were elsewhere and that he wasn't paying any attention to his strategies. And he was right. Graham couldn't stop thinking about Holly. Something was gnawing at the back of his mind.

Something that suggested that he had met her somewhere, sometime, in the past. However he didn't have a clue where and when that might have been, and since he wouldn't concentrate on what he was doing, the senator asked him to put the game up so that they could just sit and talk for a while. Graham was only too glad to oblige. During the course of the conversation, he succeeded in making his friend feel better and was able to keep his mind off this young woman who seemed to have bewitched him for some reason.

Chapter 12

"Horse thief!" Margaret O'Mally screamed at the man as he climbed into his pick-up truck. "You're nothing but a common horse thief!" Margaret's red curls bounced as she stomped her booted foot onto the dry, hard ground of the courtyard. The man ignored her outburst as he drove the truck slowly down the long, narrow lane, pulling the old trailer that contained the thoroughbred, and leaving a cloud of dust behind him.

Margaret's eyes were brimming with tears and she could no longer see her beautiful stallion clearly as she watched the horse and trailer disappear around a bend of the drive. She wasn't shedding those tears because of her attachment to the animal, but because she'd had to sell such a valuable stallion so cheaply, and she now rubbed at her eyes angrily with the back of one dainty hand. She'd had to let the animal go at a considerable loss because not many people could afford such an expensive toy in these economic times. The buyer had been able to tell by the condition of the property that Margaret was in dire need of cash, and he had taken advantage of the situation, by offering her next to nothing for the valuable horse. Margaret, of course, knew all this, but was helpless to do anything about it.

The money, what little she'd received, would allow her to survive a little longer, but what a life it would be. Her staff had left long ago. They had been loyal to her far longer than she'd deserved; probably more for the sake of her parents then the spoiled young woman. But they'd not received any wages for some time, and they finally had to seek work elsewhere if they themselves wanted to survive.

Only Elliott, the ancient horse trainer, had stayed on. As long as he had something to eat and a roof over his head, he was happy. Besides, he didn't want to desert the remaining horses. He'd cried just now when he'd had to watch Soldier being hauled away. And his had been real tears of sorrow. Now he was doubly worried because he knew that Margaret would hardly waste what little money she had on the rest of his beloved animals. Actually, he'd been the one to buy their feed, having done so for several weeks now. He'd used up almost all of his meager savings, but he couldn't bear to see the animals suffer.

The old man shook his head as he tottered back to the stable. She'd been such a cute little girl, had Margaret, but he'd thought all along that her parents had overly indulged their only child. "Spoiled her rotten," he murmured now.

Margaret in no way acknowledged what the old man was doing for her or her horses. She had her own problems and, as always, didn't consider anyone else's. The current one was breakfast. She'd never had to fix a meal before and didn't have the vaguest idea how to proceed. Being this helpless was something this young woman had not experienced before, at least not to this extent.

Of course, she would never admit that the situation she now found herself in was mostly her own fault. She was angry with Abel Smith instead, blaming the banker for all of her problems. She felt that her name alone should have been good enough for him to loan her the money she needed. After all, she was an O'Mally.

Thinking about the man reminded her of his suggestion. It might not be a bad idea to visit Michael VanDorn on his farm and throw out some strong hints that she was thinking of selling the ranch. She knew that, even if he showed an interest, he wouldn't offer her much for the property, considering the sad condition it was currently in. The money he might offer her could be enough, though, to pay off her debts and allow her to go on with her life. And then she wouldn't have to bother to come back to this godforsaken piece of ground. She would be rid of the ranch for good.

Not once did she give it a thought that this had been her childhood home, as it had been the home of her parents, who had lived here throughout their marriage until the accident had taken them away from her long before their time. Nor did she give it a thought how she would continue her life without an income. Worrying about the future was not Margaret's style.

Right now she had other thoughts that, as usual, revolved around herself. She was beginning to think that the only way she would be able to continue her former lifestyle would be to find a rich, old man who would marry her. That way all of her problems would be taken care of once and for all. Hands on hips she stood near the large picture window. She tried to think of someone who would meet her requirements. Off-hand nobody came to mind. Most of the men she knew were either married, too young, or hangers-on like she had been, with little money of their own. Then she remembered one man who might fit the bill. He was tremendously rich, but also very old, much too old for her, she thought. Her stomach felt queasy at the thought of being married to someone that ancient, and having to sleep next to him. No, she'd have to come up with someone better than that. The old geezer would be her very last resort.

She decided to forget about breakfast for now, and wondered, instead, how she would get to the VanDorn farm. Her car had been sold even before she'd had to let Soldier go. The only vehicle left on the ranch was the run-down, beat up jeep her former foreman had used to get around in. She shuddered. There was no way she would allow herself to be seen driving that decrepit old thing. Arriving at the VanDorn farm in that old wreck would definitely draw attention to her desperate circumstances. No, she'd walk first. Still standing near the window, she noticed old Elliott as he crossed the yard, which reminded her of the horses she still owned. Although not nearly as valuable as Soldier, she remembered one, Pegasus, as a decent riding horse. She would ride to the VanDorn farm and Michael wouldn't be any the wiser about her situation. Sitting astride a horse would make her look dignified and, perhaps, even a little aristocratic.

Elliott didn't like it at all that Margaret had chosen Pegasus, his favorite after Soldier, to use for her ride this morning. She was well known for her callous, almost cruel treatment of the animals, but Elliott was afraid to argue with his mistress as he still regarded her, even though she hadn't paid him in months. He feared she would make him leave and the horses would be left untended.

When she ordered him, harshly, to saddle Pegasus, he obeyed. It was inconceivable for Margaret to even think about saddling her own horse. It didn't bother her in the least that she owed the old man a substantial amount of money in back wages. As long as he was living on her ranch, he was expected to follow orders. And she wouldn't hesitate for one minute to dismiss him if he didn't do what she ordered, even if that left her without any help at all. When Margaret had one of her tantrums, she never stopped to think of the consequences.

As she rode along, her mind was already tuned to the VanDorn farm and Michael. She paid little attention to the beautiful Texas countryside, nor did she bother, for once, to torture the horse by digging her spurs into his sides. Her mind was preoccupied with her problems and how to best approach Michael -- how to make it difficult for him to refuse to help her.

It had been several years since she'd seen the young man. Back then he'd been a gangly, skinny teenager, while she herself had not yet entered her teen years, having barely reached the age of twelve. But in her girlish fantasies he'd been very handsome and he'd been her first serious crush.

Senator VanDorn and Margaret's father had liked

each other from the time they'd first met. They might have become good friends had the VanDorn's spent more time on their Texas farm, but they preferred the cooler climate up north. The farm was run by a very efficient manager, and Margaret remembered that the VanDorns only visited their property occasionally to check on how things were going.

After Margaret's parents had died when she was twenty, Drew VanDorn had offered to show her the ropes so she would be able to run the ranch. But she hadn't been interested. She'd intended to run things her way, which was to let the foreman take care of any of the work, a word that wasn't in Margaret's vocabulary anyway. In any case, she wasn't about to let anyone else tell her what to do.

The senator had been offended, not so much by her refusal of his offer, but by the way she'd gone about it. Margaret had always lacked a sense of diplomacy. Thinking only of herself, she gave little consideration for the feelings of others. After that incident, there hadn't been any further contact between the neighbors, partly because the young woman spent little time on her ranch, preferring to travel the world and letting the foreman worry about the business of managing her property.

Now Margaret was about to see Michael again, and she wondered how he would receive her. She slowed her pace, admitting to herself that it was conceivable that he might ask her to leave his farm. She certainly wasn't expecting to be greeted with open arms, even if it was Michael and not the senator whom she'd be facing.

There wasn't a soul stirring on the farm and around its buildings when Margaret finally arrived there after a long, hot ride. The farmhands were probably out working in the fields, she thought. Then she heard two men talking in quiet voices. Sitting astride the horse, she was able to see through an un-curtained window. Two men seemed to be absorbed in going over the accounting books.

Michael had decided that morning that it was time

for him to return to Seven Oaks to see how his father was doing, and to find out if Holly had changed her attitude toward him. Before he left the farm, he'd wanted to make sure everything was in order. With his foreman next to him, their heads bent over the figures, Michael thought he heard the neighing of a horse.

Pegasus had gotten the scent of some nearby mares in his nostrils, and Margaret had her hands full, trying to calm him. When Michael saw that the young woman was in trouble, he ran outside to give her a helping hand. Talking quietly to the animal, he stroked its proudly raised neck until it calmed down.

Minutes after seeing Michael, Margaret had her second crush on him. He looked so handsome with his narrow hips incased in tight jeans. His shirt, unbuttoned to his waist, showed his muscular chest, which was covered with light brown curls. Although his face was attractive, too, Margaret was more interested in the body.

Michael didn't notice the looks Margaret was giving him. "A wonderful animal," he remarked, still stroking the horse which was standing quite still now.

"Michael?" Margaret decided she'd better make sure that this was her childhood hero.

"You know me?" The young man looked up at her, surprise showing in his eyes.

"There was a time when we knew each other quite well," was Margaret's quick retort. "I'd like to renew that friendship."

Michael looked at her again, still confused. Margaret threw her head back, her red curls gleaming in the bright Texas sun, and laughed.

"Margaret O'Mally," she jogged his memory. "It has been a while since we've seen each other. I wore my hair a little differently in those days. And I think I had a few freckles at the time, too."

"Margaret!" Michael's voice rose in surprise. "A little brat with braided pig tails if I remember correctly." Michael grinned in response. "Yes, it's been a while since we last saw each other."

"You *do* remember." Margaret laughed again. "Did you know that back then I was terribly in love with you?"

The woman disconcerted Michael. She was bewitchingly beautiful. She was also an enigma. She certainly bore little resemblance to the Margaret he remembered. Michael was almost sorry that her allure left him cold. Any other time, before he'd met Holly, the promising smile might have attracted him. But now, not one minute of the day passed that he wasn't thinking of Holly and at the same time constantly asking himself what he had done wrong to make her turn against him so suddenly.

Margaret, of course, knew nothing of the thoughts going through Michael's head. She felt as though she'd suddenly been freed of a heavy burden. She forgot about her worries. She forgot about her plans to marry a rich old man; here was a rich young and handsome man who was a great deal more preferable. She could stop looking for a way out of her financial troubles, because she was sure she'd found it. But first she had to find out one important thing.

Not having acquired any diplomacy in the intervening years, she asked him point-blank, "Say, Michael, are you married?"

Still sitting astride her horse and having to look down at Michael, she failed to see the sadness that showed in his face when he answered her question.

"No," was all he could get out. In his sorrow, he never thought to ask himself why she was so interested in his marital status.

Margaret couldn't help but gloat when she heard the good news. She was now determined to become the next mistress of Seven Oaks, even though she had never seen the manor -- had only heard the senator describe it to her parents. She simply knew that it had to be a grand old house. And she was filled with so much self-importance that she had no doubt that she would succeed in capturing

A Mother's Sins

Michael's hand, if not his heart.
    Nothing mattered but the money anyway.

Chapter 13

"I'm going to take your case!"

Richard Storm placed the papers he had been studying in a neat stack in front of him, absentmindedly lining up the edges with the bottom and side of his desk calendar. He examined his new client who was sitting across from him in an old, but comfortable easy chair. Although not exactly fidgeting, the man seemed ill at ease. Richard did not attribute that to a guilty conscience but to the fact that the man evidently did not have much experience with lawyers or the law as a whole. In addition the poor man was probably worried that he might have to give up his long-time companion, his toy terrier, Heidi, who had lived with him since the dog had been a puppy. He had recently been told that animals would no longer be allowed in the apartment house were he lived.

Richard knew that any of the tenants living in the apartment who had owned a pet before the rule had been made, would be able to keep the pets under a grandfather clause. There was nothing the landlord could do about it. It was now only a matter of going before a judge and explaining the situation.

The young lawyer turned his attention back to his client, realizing his client had been talking to him -- asking a question.

"Do you really think there's a chance we'll win?" The elderly, gray-haired man drew his still-black eyebrows together in a frown. "The company who owns the apartment house is huge and has a lot of resources. They will be hard to beat," he added.

"I wouldn't worry." Richard stood up and extended

A Mother's Sins

his hand. "You have the law on your side and you did nothing wrong by keeping your little dog. There isn't anything they can do."

The two men shook hands before Richard led the other man toward the door, stopping on the way to scoop up the papers from his desk.

"I'll get in touch with you as soon as we have a court date."

After the client had left, Richard handed the documents to his secretary who looked at him curiously. Although her boss was generally in good spirits, he seemed to be even more upbeat today.

"You seem particularly cheerful today, Mr. Storm. Is there, perhaps a special reason, something that we might celebrate?"

Richard looked at her, surprised that his feelings were so obvious to others. He'd been in a wonderful mood ever since his evening with Holly, but he hadn't realized that it showed this much. Of course, Jenny was always ready to party and might just be looking for a good excuse to do so.

"I feel great," he grinned. And, as though to prove it to her, he leaned over the desk and gave the stunned woman a hearty kiss on the cheek. She was still blushing when the young receptionist looked in her direction, having heard the loud smacking sound of the kiss. However, she did not share the other woman's embarrassment when their boss threw her a kiss before he returned to his office, closing the connecting door behind him. Kathy rather wished it had been she who had received the real kiss, and she would have preferred it to be on her mouth.

"I'll bet you next week's paycheck that our boss has gone and fallen in love," Jenny couldn't resist remarking after she knew the door was closed and Richard could no longer hear her.

The receptionist didn't look happy at that pronouncement. She had adored Richard Storm ever since she had first set eyes on him when she'd come to his office to apply for a job, and she'd been overjoyed when she'd actually been hired. Now she was certain that Jenny had guessed correctly -- that there was a woman somewhere in the wings. Richard must have fallen in love sometime during the last few days, she thought. It was a pity. Kathy mourned that she hadn't been picked by Richard as the woman in his life. The two of them would make such a nice couple.

Richard didn't give his receptionist a second thought after he'd returned to his office. He didn't have a clue about her feelings for him. His thoughts were filled with Holly. He was still savoring his time with her. But despite the fact that he couldn't get his mind off her, he decided to stay out of touch for a while. He'd sensed that she didn't have the same feelings about him that he had for her, so he'd decided to give her some space. He was hoping that, if he didn't push her, she would come around.

However, several days passed and there hadn't been a word from her. Deciding that the wait was becoming actually painful for him, he made up his mind to go see her after all. For all he knew, that old saying "Out of Sight, out of Mind" might just be playing against him if he did not soon remind her that he was still around.

Even though one of his court cases had lasted longer than anticipated the next day, and the young attorney was running behind schedule, and he additionally had another appointment coming up, he decided to give Holly a quick call first. He dialed the number for Seven Oaks. Holly herself answered the phone.

"Are you free this evening?" As usual, he didn't beat around the bush and came right out with why he'd called. "I would like to see you again."

Holly hesitated. The call had been totally unexpected and she wasn't sure what to say. Still debating if she should agree to his proposal, she jumped at his voice when he loudly inquired.

"Are you there?"

Basically she wouldn't mind going out with the

young attorney again; however, she wasn't sure how to tell him that she felt nothing more than friendship for him, without hurting his feelings. She thought that the time they'd spent together had been fun. She certainly didn't want to get his hopes up and see him disappointed later on. But, as much as she liked the manor house and her work there, she sometimes longed to spend time with someone closer to her in age. Both the senator and the housekeeper were in the habit of retiring to their rooms quite early which forced Holly to have to spend her evenings alone, and she often had to come up with ideas to amuse herself. She'd never been very interested in television and she had not developed much skill in needlework. Although she had done some embroidery at her mother's sick bed just to pass the time, she did not have the patience to do a good job with the stitches. That left reading, and, although the manor library was well stocked, many of the volumes she'd found there were anything but interesting, having to do mostly with politics.

"You still haven't answered me." Richard sounding a little worried.

"I accept your invitation."

Holly at last made up her mind, surprising the young lawyer. After all, what could it hurt? Richard was an adult and should be able to handle it when she told him the truth about her feelings, or rather lack of them, for him.

I'm glad I decided to call her, Richard thought to himself. I think I did the right thing by reminding her that I am still around. Maybe she is starting to like me after all.

"Wonderful," he almost whooped into the phone. "How about this evening?" He wasn't going to give her time to change her mind after all this.

Holly still wasn't sure she was doing the right thing in going out with Richard again. She wanted to remain his friend, but her feelings simply went no deeper than that and she hoped to get an opportunity to explain this to him without losing his friendship and without hurting him in the process.

Richard's car pulled up in front of the manor punctually at the time he'd agreed to pick her up, just as he'd done on their first date. This time he drove her to a nearby city and took her to an elegant restaurant. Since he hadn't mentioned where he would be taking her, she was glad she had dressed appropriately for the occasion in a lightweight, beige linen dress with a little short sleeved jacket to match.

The hostess seated them at a small table hidden in a corner behind some huge potted plants. The waiter brought a bottle of wine, which Richard had apparently ordered in advance. It occurred to Holly that he must have been pretty sure of himself, certain that she would not turn his invitation down.

A small band was playing romantic tunes on an elevated stage at the other side of the room. This, too, seemed to have been planned. The music was just loud enough to be heard, but not so loud as to make conversation impossible.

"I would like to say something to you," Richard reached for Holly's hand. "I have fallen in love with you," he continued quickly, not giving her a chance to interrupt.

This, of course, was the moment Holly had been dreading. She did, however, resist her first impulse to withdraw her hand from his.

"I like you, Richard," she said, looking straight into his dark brown eyes. "I like you very much, but I don't feel that spark that would indicate that there is love between us. I would be extremely happy if we could be friends. But that's all it can be. There can't ever be more between us."

Richard anticipated her reaction and was not as hurt by it as he'd expected. He even managed a smile. However, he was not the kind of person to give up easily.

"OK," he said cheerfully. "We'll be friends. We'll see what happens later. I can wait. But I am also certain that, some day, you will fall in love with me -- and much deeper for having waited so long. I will give you time."

Ursula Turner

Chapter 14

When Holly came down for breakfast the next morning, she found herself face to face with Michael. Her heart almost stopped.

"Holly!" He was not able to hide his feelings completely when he said her name. But he quickly regained control of himself. "Up so early?"

It took a little longer for the young woman to recover from the surprise of seeing Michael so unexpectedly, and to pull herself together. After that first shock her heart had started pounding so hard, she knew it had to show through her blouse. It was difficult to keep her emotions from showing. Of course, she hadn't known that Michael had returned from his trip to Texas.

"It's nice to see you back," she finally managed to respond to his words, her voice scratchy and sounding forced. She didn't dare let him know in any way how she really felt, although he couldn't help but realize that she was not acting naturally.

They stood silent for a moment; caught up in their own thoughts. There was so much they wanted to say to each other. Instead, their silence filled the room more than words ever could.

The tension was broken by the senator's hearty voice, "Michael!" He hurried toward his son and put his hands on the younger man's shoulders, giving them a squeeze. "I'm surprised to see you." He gave Holly a quick smile before turning back to his son. "When did you get back?"

So the senator hadn't known about Michael's return either, Holly thought.

"We arrived some time during the night," Michael answered his father's question. I think it was around one or two o'clock and we didn't want to disturb you at such an ungodly hour." Michael didn't see why it should be important when he'd arrived; he was more concerned about his father's health, and had all sorts of questions. "How are you feeling?" he asked. "Are you sure you should be up? Don't you think you ought to lie down.

"Don't you start in now," the senator grumbled. "I feel fine." He sounded somewhat absentminded when he gave his answer and his grumble didn't sound as fierce as usual. He had noticed something odd Michael had said and had to find out what it meant. "Did I hear you say "we"? What does that mean? Did you bring company?"

Michael fidgeted a little, not knowing how his father would take the news, "I hope you don't mind, but I did bring a guest. You probably remember Margaret O'Mally."

The senator nodded. "The beautiful young lady from the Texas ranch. I remember her well." He wasn't very happy about having this particular woman as a guest, but he refrained from showing his feelings for the present. "How did you manage to hook up with her? From what I've heard, she's seldom at home."

It was impossible for Michael to tell by his father's expression how he really felt about having Margaret as a guest. But he had a feeling that the older man wasn't very pleased, although, Michael knew he would be too polite to say anything.

Holly had managed to sip some of her coffee while listening to the men. Her heart had skipped a beat when she learned about Michael's guest, but his next words had a somewhat calming effect.

"Margaret plans to sell her ranch." Michael looked at his father to see what the other man's reaction would be to what he had to say next. "That's why I came back earlier than planned. I thought we might consider buying it since it borders on our property. I wanted to discuss this with you in person."

"I happen to know that the O'Mally estate is not in very good shape," VanDorn remarked. He couldn't wholly hide some of his scorn at the young woman's lack of management.

"Correct," Michael agreed. "Margaret didn't hide the fact that she knows nothing about running a ranch and has no interest in learning. The price she quoted is quite reasonable, especially since the horses she still owns are included."

The senator raised his head and began to show some interest.

"The horses! That's a different story. The O'Malley's have long been recognized for raising some of the greatest racehorses that exist in this country."

Michael nodded, "And one of the better ones is still in Margaret's possession. I've seen her ride it myself." He looked at his father. "So, do you agree that we should purchase the ranch?"

"I'll trust your judgment, son." The older man still tired easily and was beginning to show it. "If you think the amount is fair, go ahead and get things rolling. But I really think you should have a look at it before you sign the final papers."

Holly was curious about Margaret O'Mally whom the senator had described as beautiful; however, she didn't get to meet her until evening.

The visitor entered the parlor with her arm hooked possessively into the crook of Michael's elbow, and, although Holly felt a tightness in her chest when she saw the two of them so apparently intimate, she had to admit that the other woman was, indeed, very beautiful.

With Margaret walking alongside Michael as she did, Holly noticed that her head only reached to the young man's shoulder. Her waist was slim and her hips tapered down to slender, but shapely legs. Her fire-red hair fell in soft curls down to her shoulders, framing a face that had been expertly made up to hide any flaws that might exist. But her lovely blue eyes narrowed when Michael introduced her to Holly.

Holly knew instinctively that Margaret O'Mally did not like her, and after Michael mentioned that Holly was his father's secretary, Margaret barely acknowledged her with a nod, ignoring Holly's outstretched hand.

Neither Drew VanDorn nor his son apparently had noticed their guest's rude behavior, so Holly thought it prudent to hide her resentment. She lowered her hand to her side and made up her mind to avoid Margaret whenever possible. She had no intention of having this snob make her feel inferior. Holly was normally slow to anger, but she had a feeling about the other woman that told her she was up to no good, and she, Holly, was certain that this had nothing to do with her own feelings for Michael.

Margaret O'Mally, on the other hand, raised her eyebrows in surprise when she saw Holly enter the dining room with the rest of the small group.

"You dine with your secretary?" she asked the senator.

Senator VanDorn showed his displeasure at her words by wrinkling his brow. "Do you have any objections?" he growled. "I appreciate Miss Snyder's company not only at work, but outside of working hours as well. And the same goes for my housekeeper, Mrs. Walters," he added, to make sure the woman from Texas knew how he felt about the situation. "She isn't here today, but when she's present, she always eats with the family."

Holly considered it demeaning, the way they were talking about her -- as though she weren't present. Even the fact that the senator had taken her side and had stood up for her didn't change her feelings. She would have loved to leave and go to her room. But then she noticed Michael's smile. It was warm and gentle and left her all soft and shaky inside. She instantly forgot the other woman's malicious behavior.

Ursula Turner

Chapter 15

"I think your father should be a little more mindful of his reputation," Margaret's high-pitched voice expressed her disapproval to perfection and allowed everyone in the vicinity to hear it clearly. Holly had decided to go to her room after dinner, but was able to hear her through the open window. "I, personally, wouldn't dream of dining with the servants."

She'd pleaded with Michael until he agreed to walk in the gardens with her after their meal was over.

Michael smiled, but didn't pay much attention to her words. It hadn't escaped his attention that his guest was quite arrogant and it, therefore, didn't surprise him to learn how she felt about people she considered beneath her. However, he knew that, as soon as their business was concluded, the young woman would be leaving and he would no longer have to listen to her unsolicited opinion.

"Perhaps you should explain to him that it hurts his dignity and possibly his standing in the community when he lowers himself to dining with the personnel." She wouldn't let the matter rest.

And Michael could no longer ignore her. "My dear Margaret, I will do no such thing. Not only would I never presume to tell my father how to conduct himself in his own house, but I happen to feel the same way he does about this subject. In addition, the people of our community think of him quite highly. I don't think he has anything to worry about in that regard."

Margaret had to bite her tongue to keep from saying what she really wanted to say. She hadn't failed to notice the looks Michael had sent in the direction of his father's secretary, and how he had smiled at her across the dinner table. His actions worried her. She'd been so certain that she'd already won Michael over, since he had invited her to Seven Oaks. Vain as she was, it had not occurred to her that he might have done so for business reasons, regardless that it had been her idea to approach him about the sale of her ranch. Somehow business never seemed to stay put for long in Margaret's pretty head. At the moment, however, she didn't feel quite so sure of herself. With the other woman so highly respected by her employers that she was allowed to eat with them could make for serious competition.

So, consequently, she was actually afraid to indicate to Michael that she was displeased with him. She felt that she'd said enough for now. She didn't want to alienate him in any way, nor did she want to put herself in a bad light. So she hooked her hand into the crook of his arm, something she seemed to feel the need to do whenever she was walking with him. She snuggled closer to him as they strolled along the graveled path, while she was trying to do her best to stay in step with him and his long legs.

"You probably think me terribly arrogant, and you're probably right -- up to a point," Margaret said by way of an explanation for her earlier words and behavior. "However, I can't help the way I was raised." She sighed deeply.

Michael laughed. Margaret's self-assessment had something disarming about it; however, he would have been shocked, had he known what was really going on in that beautiful head of hers. He had no way of knowing that this young woman was a schemer, always trying to see what was in it for her in any given situation.

"I don't think your father likes me," she broke into his thoughts, changing the subject. "He has probably never forgiven me for not accepting his help after my parents died."

"I don't believe that for a minute," Michael said with conviction, knowing that his father did not carry a grudge, but also knowing that there were other reasons why Drew VanDorn had no use for Margaret O'Mally. "My father is probably acting grumpy right now because he doesn't feel well, and also because the doctor won't let him get back to his work." Michael felt that he had to justify his father's treatment of Margaret in some way.

"Nevertheless, it might be better if I left as soon as possible," Margaret persisted, squeezing a few tears from her eyes, tears that slowly rolled down her lovely cheeks.

She waited anxiously for Michael's response. He reacted exactly the way she had hoped.

"Nonsense! I don't think it would hurt for you to stick around a little longer," he replied as she had thought he would. "At least stay until the Harvest Festival. I'm sure Dad won't mind, as long as you don't aggravate him. I'm a little worried that it probably isn't too good for his heart if he excites himself."

True to her nature Margaret ignored Michael's remarks about his father's health. The senator's medical condition wasn't something she cared to worry about. But Michael had said something that was of real interest to her.

"A festival?" She repeated Michael's words, excitement in her voice. She loved parties of any kind and missed them sorely, now that she no longer could afford to give any herself.

"The Harvest Festival is a tradition at Seven Oaks. It takes place on the first Sunday in October, and on that day it is never cold, even if we had frost before that date. The temperature is always comfortable on that day, and it never rains."

Margaret didn't question Michael's words about the weather. There were more important things to think about. She was anxious to hear more about the festival. She especially wanted to know whom the VanDorns planned to invite and, of course, what the ladies would be wearing.

Michael placed his arm around her slim shoulders

and, dutifully, answered her questions to the best of his ability. Neither of them suspected that they were being watched.

Holly was standing at the window of her room and was observing the couple's every move with burning eyes. She could no longer hear what they were saying, since the two young people had moved out of earshot as they walked, but Holly had already ceased trying to fool herself. She was terribly jealous. It didn't matter any more that Michael might be her brother, or at the very least, her half brother. All that mattered was the fact that she loved him with all her heart. And now it was too late. He had found someone else.

She might have had an easier time of accepting her fate, had she been able to like Margaret O'Mally. And she was totally convinced that Michael would never be happy with this haughty, cold and selfish young woman. Holly felt that, should he marry her, he would regret it for the rest of his life.

She watched as Michael placed his arm around Margaret's shoulders and walked with her along the path, farther away from the house. She finally turned away, when tears of disappointment distorted her vision. At any rate, she found it impossible to watch their progress any longer. It hurt more than any pain she had ever experienced, and there was nothing she could do to make the situation bearable.

Ursula Turner

Chapter 16

Margaret O'Mally was determined to reach her goal of becoming Mrs. Michael VanDorn and that this fact would be known to all the people who mattered no later than the Harvest Festival. At this point she didn't care what was going on between Michael and that silly secretary of his father's. It didn't really matter. She, Margaret, would become Michael's wife, and the festival would be the perfect occasion to announce their engagement.

However, hard as she tried, she couldn't seem to get anywhere with the young heir to Seven Oaks. He gave absolutely no indication that he had an interest in her in a romantic way and although he continued to treat her very pleasantly and was unfailingly friendly to her, he did not pledge his undying love to her. It was so frustrating, especially since she so desperately needed to reach this goal of marriage to Michael. Having traveled to Seven Oaks had not relieved her of the burden of overdue bills. They had managed to follow her all the way here, and some of them frightened her with their threatening content. Of course, she couldn't possibly tell Michael about this problem. She was still under the impression that he thought her fairly well off, and she determined not to mention her indebtedness until after they were safely married.

Margaret, who was used to getting her own way most of the time, was beginning to worry about Michael's casual treatment of her. Normally she would have told herself that Michael just needed a little more time to get used to the idea of marriage. However, like a gnawing toothache, there was that other woman -- that lowly secretary. Margaret couldn't forget the special way Michael had looked at this Holly or whatever silly name she claimed as her own. The jealous redhead had certainly noticed his eyes, full of longing, a longing he had unsuccessfully tried to hide.

Michael loved his father's secretary; that much Margaret had been able to determine in the short time she'd been given to observe the couple. What she could not understand was what was stopping the two from getting together, from dating, from becoming a so-called "item". She would have liked to discuss this puzzling behavior with Michael, if only to satisfy her curiosity, but then thought better of it. It might not be a good idea to stir things up.

One day, the two women bumped into each other while in the city. Holly, who had the afternoon off, was shopping for a gown to wear at the Harvest Festival. Since she hadn't had any plans of going to any big parties while at the manor and had no occasion to attend any for some time at home, her wardrobe did not contain anything suitable for that kind of festivity. She was standing in front of a full-length mirror looking at herself critically while trying on a silvery-blue, shimmering creation the saleslady had recommended, when Margaret stalked into the elegant clothing store.

"It looks like we had the same idea," she observed in the superior voice she apparently saved for Holly and others whom she considered beneath her. "Are you sure that one isn't a little out of your league?" She stabbed a stiff finger, tipped with a crimson colored nail, toward the dress Holly was wearing.

"Why don't you let me worry about that?" Holly didn't think it was any of the other woman's business what kind of clothing she chose to wear. But Margaret kept it up, taunting her and, finally managed to spoil Holly's afternoon off, and the young secretary felt no longer in the mood for shopping. She was actually considering skipping the festival altogether if it meant she wouldn't have to put up with the temperamental redhead. But then she reconsidered and decided not to give the other woman the satisfaction of spoiling the party for her.

Margaret glared at her, "I know you live in the manor house and that the senator puts up with you at meal times. But do you really expect to be invited to the Harvest Festival?"

"The senator has already invited me," Holly answered quietly, although her lips trembled slightly. Her apparent calm seemed to infuriate the other woman, who stepped closer to Holly -- so close, in fact, that Holly could see the small, blue veins throbbing in her temples. "I must say, you are good at this," Margaret hissed through clenched teeth. "But even if you have fooled the senator with your apparent innocence, you best leave your fingers off Michael."

For a moment Holly was speechless. How had Margaret learned she was interested in Michael, she wondered? Was it that obvious? Did something like that really show? Or were the other women simply guessing?

"Don't you worry, Ms. O'Mally," she finally managed to say through stiff lips, outwardly still calm, but trembling on the inside, whether from anger or plain frustration at her awkward situation, she did not know. "I don't have the slightest intention of getting involved with Michael VanDorn," she finished. "And now, If you'll excuse me..."

Under the circumstances, Holly walked back to the dressing room with a sense of dignity. Once inside, she had to lean against the closed door for a moment. It took her a while to calm down, but she did not want Margaret to know how much her ugly words had upset her. Her insides remained quivery for some time, and her knees would hardly hold her up. After taking a few deep breaths, she yanked the dress off, having lost all the joy she had felt when first seeing herself in the mirror with it on. As soon

A Mother's Sins

as she was back in her own clothes, she left the store without looking around to see if the other woman was still there.

Once on the sidewalk, she couldn't decide whether she was ready to return to her rooms in the manor house. Right now she was in no mood to see anybody and she didn't want anybody she knew to see her. So she continued walking, not even glancing into the many shop windows she was passing.

Since Michael's return, her feelings were all mixed up. Sometimes she wished she had not discovered that Bill Snyder wasn't her real father, and she regretted finding the paper that had led her to Seven Oaks. Then she would never have met Michael and experienced the pain that was continuously with her. Instead she would probably be living peacefully somewhere by herself, without any of these unsettling feelings or the constant ache in her heart. Holly tried to ignore the inner voice that kept whispering that she would probably feel very lonely in that scenario.

I feel lonely now, she thought, in spite of the people I see every day. A feeling that had gotten stronger, oddly enough, since Michael had returned. She hated to admit, even to herself, that she missed his companionship terribly. Every time she saw him, she realized how much she loved him and how little chance there was that this love would ever be fulfilled.

Deep in thought, Holly kept walking along the sidewalk. She jumped when she, unexpectedly, felt a hand on her shoulder. When she turned her head, she was looking straight into Richard Storm's grinning face.

"I was just thinking about you," he claimed, "and here you are. Surely that's not a coincidence. I think it's a sign. I just finished seeing a client and I'm starving. Would you join me in a hearty lunch? You look like you could use something nourishing."

To be around Richard with his constant optimism and cheerful disposition made Holly feel better. She quickly agreed to his offer. His face lit up with new hope.

Chapter 17

"How much longer will Miss O'Mally be staying with us?" Senator VanDorn didn't sound very happy as he questioned his son.

Michael was surprised. Had Margaret been correct in her assumption that his father didn't like her?

"Why do you want to know? What do you have against her?" He decided to be blunt and find out how his father really felt about the young woman.

"More to the point," the senator grumbled," what do *you* see in her?"

"She is funny and intelligent and, besides, I like her candor."

"Careful," the senator warned. "I don't believe that Miss O'Mally is as frank as you seem to think. I decided to have her investigated and have discovered that she is practically penniless; is, in fact, up to her neck in debt. She has managed to squander all of her sizeable inheritance within just a few years."

Michael was furious. "How could you be so insensitive? I can't believe that you had Margaret spied on!" he berated his father.

The senator remained calm, "I like to know with whom I'm dealing when it comes to making any large investments such as purchasing the land she has for sale."

"You've known the O'Malley's for a number of years," Michael pointed out.

"I knew Margaret's father quite well and her mother to some extent," Drew VanDorn corrected his son. "Mr. O'Mally was an honest, hard working man whom I respected highly. His daughter doesn't seem to have inherited any of her father's good qualities, and what I do know of her tends to leave a bitter taste in my mouth."

"She was very young when her father died," Michael wasn't giving up that easily. "Perhaps she couldn't handle the management of the ranch at such a young age."

"You were off to college at the time, so you wouldn't know, but I tried to help her with the running of the ranch. I tried to teach her a few of the things she needed to know, but she turned my help down flat. She said she wasn't in the least interested and made it clear that she would not soil her pretty little hands. She also informed me that she had a foreman who was being paid to take care of the dirty work."

"I did know about that, and I still think that she was probably too young for all that responsibility," Michael retorted.

"It makes me worry, listening to you trying to defend her actions. Have you fallen in love with Margaret O'Mally?" The senator's frown had deepened.

"Now I understand what you're getting at," Michael grinned. "Would you have any objections?"

The look Drew VanDorn gave his son did not hide the love he felt for him. "I want you to be happy," he told him. "It doesn't matter if the woman you plan to marry is wealthy or not. What's important is that you love her and that she loves you in return. My concern lies with Margaret's feelings for you. I fear she is like the women we discussed the other day. She may be only after your money since she has none of her own now."

Michael was touched by his father's words. "I don't love Margaret O'Mally," he quickly assured him. "I only feel sorry for her. You need not worry that I am romantically attached to her."

Drew VanDorn shook his head, "I've always been able to read people to some extent. I'm convinced Miss O'Mally's reason to visit us is not only for the purpose of selling her ranch. I think she wants it all. I don't think she'll give up until she has you, too."

Michael laughed out loud, "You certainly have strange ideas. But I know you have to be wrong. In fact, Margaret had already planned to leave. I talked her into staying for the Harvest Festival." The young man decided not mention that their visitor had noticed the senator's dislike for her.

"I hope you know what you're doing." With one more worried look at his son, VanDorn left the room.

Michael was sure that Margaret didn't care for him any more than he cared for her, so he wasn't too concerned about what his father had said. He enjoyed her company because she made him laugh, something he was sorely in need of right now. It helped to have something or someone take his mind of his big problem, which, of course, was the way Holly continued acting toward him.

He had given up trying to figure out why she was constantly avoiding him. However, each time he saw her, he felt a sharp pain in his chest. He loved her more than he would have thought it was possible for one person to love another, more than anything in the world, and sometimes, when they accidentally happened to look into each other's eyes, he was sure she felt the same way about him. That's what made the situation so intolerable. If she would only confide in him, tell him what had brought on the sudden change of heart she was displaying so cruelly toward him.

Yet, Michael had decided not to push her -- to be patient instead. Perhaps, at some point, Holly would decide on her own to tell him why, after being so friendly at their first meeting, she'd done such a complete turnabout and wanted absolutely nothing to do with him, would hardly speak to him. He hoped that, once he knew the reason, he might be able to change her mind about whatever was keeping her at such a distance.

But sometimes, especially at night when he couldn't sleep for thinking about Holly, and longing for her, he broke into a cold sweat when he considered that he might have waited too long and might end up losing her for good.

At such moments he had all he could do to resist the temptation to run to her room, take her in his arms, even if she resisted, and tell her again and again how much he loved her, and to repeat those words until she at last confided in him and told him what was bothering her, what was causing her to back away from him.

Only one thing kept him from taking this desperate step. He was afraid he'd get her so upset and mixed up that she would leave the manor on impulse, and he would not ever see her again.

On one such night, or rather late evening, he was standing at the window of his room, when he saw a car stop in front of the house. He immediately recognized it as belonging to Richard Storm, his father's attorney and his own former classmate. At first he didn't think anything of it and was just about to turn away. Richard was probably here to see his father about some legal matter, although it was a little late in the day for that. But he knew that the two of them had never been sticklers in observing office hours. Then, out of the corner of his eye, he saw Richard get out of the car, walk around to the passenger side, open the door and give Holly his hand to help her get out of the vehicle.

That's when Michael did turn away. He was beginning to realize that he'd been fooling himself all along when he had thought Holly had feelings for him. How could he have been so stupid? She'd apparently found a man to her liking in Richard Storm, the VanDorn family lawyer.

Ursula Turner

Chapter 18

Since it was an unusually warm day for this time of year, just as Michael had promised, Holly was wearing an ankle-length, sleeveless dress of pale beige satin with thin spaghetti straps. A medium brown, narrow belt of the same material encircled her slender waist. The sandals she wore, which had two-inch heels, matched the brown of the belt perfectly. Since her job included room and board, in addition to her receiving a handsome salary from the senator, she had decided to splurge just this once and purchase an ensemble that cost a little more than what she normally spent on clothing. But she wanted to be able to blend in with the other guests. The dress, in its simplicity, made her look like a million dollars, at least Michael thought so and he couldn't keep his eyes off her as she approached the small group of guests already assembled in the great hall.

"You look beautiful." The young man couldn't help himself -- he had to tell her. Not only Holly, but also Margaret, who was standing next to him, noticed the wistful note in his voice.

The Texas ranch woman's eyes narrowed to slits as she cast a hateful look toward Holly. Margaret's dress was created from a glittery red material that clashed with the color of her hair. But it was apparent that she knew this and had dressed this way simply to get the attention she so craved. It didn't seem to matter to her how she had to go about this. She hadn't, however, counted on Holly's natural beauty and dignity that drew everyone's interest, that, and the fact that not many of the guests had met the quiet, pretty young woman and wondered who she was.

A Mother's Sins

Margaret, on the other hand had made sure that everyone knew who she was by insisting that Michael introduce her to guests as soon as they arrived.

"Thank you," Holly replied to Michael's compliment, rewarding him with a friendly smile before she turned to Richard Storm who was her date for the Harvest Festival. The young attorney had stood patiently at her side, waiting for his turn to shake his old classmate's hand. He received only a halfhearted, limp handshake and an absent nod of the head, however. Puzzled at his friend's strange behavior, particularly when he was accompanied by such a stunning redhead to whom Richard had not yet been introduced, he and Holly strolled out to the patio to meet some of the other people.

Michael stared after the couple with burning eyes as they slowly strolled toward the ornate railing that edged the patio on its three sides away from the house, leaving a wide opening for the stone stairs that led into the garden.

"A cute couple," Margaret remarked with false friendliness, hooking her arm into Michael's, as had become her habit. She, too, had watched Holly and Richard walk away, but with quite different emotions than Michael's. For just an instant she could feel him stiffen at her words.

"Yes," he at last squeezed out, his voice barely a whisper. Then, trying to convince himself that none of it mattered, he followed Margaret who, promptly, led him in the opposite direction. She was already acting like the lady of the house by making small-talk with all the guests, whether they cared to hear what she had to say or not. The redhead seemed to have convinced herself that this was part of her duty as Michael's date.

Michael managed to hide the raw pain he felt throughout the next several hours. He didn't want anyone to know how much he was hurting deep inside. So, he chatted with guests, laughed at their jokes and told his own as well, acting all the while as though he were having the time of his life. But again and again he glanced around to see if he could catch a glimpse of Holly and Richard.

Margaret never left his side, but was quite unhappy that she hadn't come even one step closer to her goal of capturing the young heir's hand, if not his heart. It didn't matter if he didn't love her. All she wanted was his money first and his name second. But her grand plans to announce their engagement at the occasion of the Harvest Festival had so far come to nothing.

On top of that, she had, just today, received a letter from Abel Smith, the banker, in which he practically demanded to hear some firm commitment on her part on how she intended to pay off her debts. He had as much as threatened her with dire consequences if he didn't hear from her soon, and she wondered if people still got thrown in jail for not paying up what they owed. It was not a pleasant thought, but short of demanding that Michael marry her, she didn't have a clue how she would pay her debts. Never having involved herself with any of the sordid business of the ranch, she had no idea how much it might be worth in its current run-down state.

The young woman was also beginning to feel some anger in addition to being a little worried, about the fact that the negotiations on the sale of her ranch to the VanDorns were dragging along so slowly. She suspected that the senator was behind this. However, she had been told that there hadn't been time to look into the situation while preparations for today's festival were in progress. She wouldn't have minded the delay, had she been assured that there would be a wedding with Michael in her future. After all, in that case it would all belong to both of them anyway.

However, she hesitated to put any kind of pressure on Michael. She had no plans of letting him know how bad her financial situation was. And while she would have initially settled for the sale of her ranch only, she now wanted nothing less than to marry the senator's son.

There was, of course, no way for her to know that her situation had been thoroughly investigated, and that father and son were well aware of her substantial debts.

A buffet, tempting guests with its numerous delicacies, had been set up on the patio. Gertrude Walters, dressed in a forest green gown, kept herself in the background while managing the entire affair, making sure everything ran smoothly. She kept an eagle eye on the catering personnel as well as on the kitchen help, and made sure none of the bowls and platters on the long, linen-draped table remained empty for long.

Later on, a band played dance music. Holly allowed Richard to lead her to the dance floor and dutifully laughed at a funny remark he whispered in her ear. She cried inside, however, when she caught a glimpse of Margaret, nestled in Michael's arms, as the two whirled around the dance floor. There was no mistaking the triumphant gleam in the other woman's green eyes when the couples passed each other.

Why did this woman hate her so? Holly wondered once again, helplessly. She must have noticed by now that, at least outwardly, Holly was showing no interest in Michael. What the young secretary couldn't know was that, with typical womanly intuition, Margaret was able to sense the tension that existed between Michael and Holly. She was certain that the two had feelings for each other that they did not allow the public to see, and Margaret was dying to know what the reason for this odd behavior was. She didn't trust this situation at all and was not going to give Michael a chance to put whatever differences the two might have, to rights.

Thinking of the last run-in with Margaret and seeing her now in such intimacy with Michael, Holly suddenly lost all desire to be at this party. Once again the other woman had her way and had spoiled Holly's bit of happiness. And this time she had managed to do so without saying one word to Holly. She asked Richard quietly to take her back to the patio, from where she could discretely slip to her rooms by walking around the house and entering through the front door. She didn't want anyone to notice that she'd left the festivities.

"Are you all right?" Richard asked concern noticeable in his voice.

"I'm fine." Holly forced herself to smile. "I just need a little fresh air."

Once outside, Richard left Holly alone for a few moments to get a drink for the two of them. Holly leaned her arms on the railing, debating if she really wanted to return to her rooms. She looked out into the gardens that had been decorated with strings of colored lanterns. Like a fairytale, she thought, only she wasn't the princess.

Suddenly Holly could no longer stand the loud voices, the laughter and the music behind her. She yearned for some quiet to get her troubling thoughts sorted out.

When Richard returned with their refreshments, Holly was gone. Frantically searching for her because he was sure there had been something bothering her and he was worried about what she might do, he couldn't find her among any of the guests. Nobody had seen her or could tell him in what direction she might have gone. He couldn't know that there was one person who'd been watching and who'd seen Holly walk into the gardens.

Chapter 19

Just as Margaret turned away from a young man who had been trying to flirt with her throughout most of the evening and whom she had been trying to discourage without success, she caught a glimpse of Michael as he was leaving the patio. He quickly disappeared into the trees that made up part of the manor grounds. Without hesitating for even a moment, and without a word of apology to the young man, who, she felt, didn't deserve one anyway, she followed the heir of this prosperous estate. She was afraid to leave him out of her sight for even one moment. With all the available, beautiful young women at the party, he might possibly find one better suited to him then she, a southerner, who had practically begged him to bring her up north to his home. And although she had only hoped, at first, that he would buy her ranch, she had set her sights much higher now. She was convinced that Michael was the one who would, somehow, rescue her from her financial nightmares, preferably by marrying her.

Michael never looked back in his rush into the woods and would have failed to see Margaret in any case since she was staying in the darker shadows under the trees. Much as she wanted to catch up with him, she first had to see what he was up to. Could he be in such a rush because he was anxious to meet someone secretly away from the manor? Could it be that Holly girl he was running after? Margaret clenched her small hands into fists until her sharp nails bit into her skin. She couldn't recall having seen the other woman recently.

Michael's whole being was focused on finding Holly. He stumbled around in the darkness under the trees, but was afraid to call her name in case she decided to run even farther into the woods.

Then he saw her!

She was standing near the bank of the small lake, and the moonlight which was reflected in the still water bathed her in an otherworldly glow.

Michael stopped and took in the breathtaking picture. To him the young woman looked almost celestial in her light-colored dress and those flaxen, shoulder-length curls that shimmered in the silvery light.

All at once, Holly sensed that she was no longer alone. She turned and was startled to find herself looking at Michael, who was now standing directly in front of her. He was so close, in fact, that she could smell the musky scent of his aftershave lotion and felt his gentle breath on her cheek.

"I love you." Michael couldn't help himself. He had to tell her. Then he pulled her into his arms. "I love you so very much." He couldn't say it often enough.

His lips sought her mouth, carefully at first, barely touching, then more forceful and full of longing.

For one instant Holly surrendered and nestled against him, while his arms were encircling her, enjoying this moment of happiness to its fullest, knowing it wouldn't -- it couldn't last. When Michael moaned softly, she regained her senses.

What am I doing? She chastised herself. She was mortified at what she'd allowed to let happen. She pushed Michael, who didn't know what was happening to him, away from herself with all the force she could muster. He looked at her helplessly as though asking, what have I done now?

"Holly, but... but I love you," he stammered, reaching for her and managing to grasp hold of one of her arms. Why did she keep changing her mind about her feelings about him? He could tell that there was something that kept her acting so strangely, something she refused to tell him for some reason. But he knew better than to ask what was bothering her, because she had not answered him before and certainly would not answer his plea now.

Holly shrugged him off, making him let go of her arm. "I'm sorry that you feel that way," she answered, her voice hoarse. "I really couldn't care less about you. You don't mean a thing to me, so please from now on I would appreciate it if you would leave me alone. My feelings for you won't ever change, so I'd be very thankful if you would quit bothering me."

They were cruel words and hurt her more than anyone would ever know, especially when she saw their effect on Michael -- the way they had wounded him. He reached toward her again, without seemingly realizing what he was doing, then let his hands drop by his side when he recognized the futility of his gesture, because Holly had turned her back on him. He couldn't know she had done this to hide her tears.

With a lost expression in his eyes, Michael watched her walk away from him. It was over -- done with before it could ever begin. The woman whom he loved more than anything on this earth would never belong to him. Nothing else mattered at this moment but that one single thought -- a thought that took possession of him.

Suddenly Margaret was standing there, as though she had replaced Holly. The woman wound both of her arms around his neck in a false effort to comfort him. She had seen everything; first full of anger, later in puzzlement, and then, when Holly had turned Michael away, with silent satisfaction. Although she'd never actually felt love for anyone, she could tell that Michael was filled with despair over his loss, and she decided to take advantage of his state of mind. She neglected to tell him that she had seen what happened. Instead she pulled him close enough to her to feel his heartbeat.

"Where have you been?" she whispered. "I missed you."

Michael didn't move. Only when her full, lush lips

touched his mouth softly did he wake up from his almost catatonic state. He reached for Margaret's shoulder and pushed her away from him, looking at her face as though he didn't know her and needed to determine who this person standing in front of him was.

"I love you, Michael," Margaret told him quietly. "I can't imagine my life without you, now that I've found you again after all these years."

Michael started to say something, but Margaret placed her soft hand on his lips. "Don't talk right now. Let me convince you that we belong together. Even our names begin with the same letter. I know you don't feel the same about me as I do for you, but we have so much time -- an entire lifetime."

"An entire lifetime...," Michael echoed and stared over Margaret's shoulder into the darkness. An eternal lifetime -- without Holly! He felt as though he could no longer bear the pain.

"I need you, Michael, and you need me." Instinctively Margaret had given voice to the right words at the right time. With his thoughts in such a muddle, Michael didn't even question what Margaret meant by them.

However, he agreed with what she had said. Yes, he thought, I do need her, and if not her than somebody who can stand by my side and comfort me. And since Margaret is already conveniently here, why not her. She seemed to be more than willing to help him dull the pain. As his wife, she could belong to him and care for him. It might as well be Margaret, he told himself; since he was now convinced that Holly would never be that someone. And so it didn't matter who it actually was.

"Could you see yourself as my wife?" he asked Margaret, but was instantly sorry he had asked the question. She couldn't have known that she had caught him in a weak moment -- which he might not have asked her this question at any other time. But it was too late now. He had asked the question and he wouldn't take it back.

Margaret's face lit up. "Oh, Michael," she breathed. "You've made me so happy."

"I don't know if you'll stay that way once you marry me," Michael warned her, "I like you, Margaret, but I want you to understand that's as far as my feelings for you will ever go."

"My love is enough for the two of us," Margaret assured him, "and I will try my best to see to it that you, also, will be happy."

It was an easy promise for her to make, especially since she had no intention of keeping it. She didn't care in the least whether Michael was happy or not. She had reached her goal and would play along with whatever Michael wanted until they had said their "I do's". A marriage to the senator's heir was all that mattered to her.

Right now, she felt, was the time to get Michael to make the final commitment, while his mind was still in this fragile emotional state. She would not get this opportunity again. Reaching for his hand, she purred.

"We should share our happiness with your guests. Everybody should know that we will belong to each other from now on." She assumed that, once the news was made public, Michael would be unable to retract his offer.

He followed her back to the manor where the party was still in full swing. They searched for his father to ask him to announce their engagement. When they, at last, found the senator sitting in the library, away from all the noise and merriment of the festivities, the young man was still in such a state of shock over losing Holly that he failed to notice how pale his father had turned on hearing the news.

"Are you sure you're doing the right thing, my boy?" The older man kept hoping that he hadn't heard them correctly.

"I'm very sure," Michael nodded his head, while avoiding his father's eyes.

A few minutes later, a drum roll alerted the guests.

"Ladies and gentlemen," the senator stood at one end of the patio facing his guests, "I have the honor," he began, hesitation noticeable in his voice. But he forced himself to smile, "and pleasure," he continued, making his voice sound stronger, "to announce the engagement of my son Michael, to Miss Margaret O'Mally heir to the O'Mally ranch in Texas."

Chapter 20

Holly made several attempts to discuss her mother with the senator during the next few weeks. Each time she built up her courage, she'd have to put it off because she was interrupted by visitors who needed to see the senator for one reason or another. She was unable to find an opportunity to be alone with him. In any case, she was still hesitant to learn the truth about her heritage, fearful of what the senator would have to tell her. In one way she was wishing that this wonderful man was her father, but on the other hand she knew that, should that be the case, it would dash her final, slim hope to be able to love Michael as anyone other than her brother. Then again, the few times she might have had an opportunity to talk with her boss, she could tell that he didn't feel well and she did not want to bother him then. So, one chance after another slipped by, and she was no closer to learning the truth than when she'd first arrived at Seven Oaks.

One evening, Richard had, once again, intended to take Holly out for dinner, but it was quite late, when he finally called. He told her, regret obvious in his voice, that an appointment with a client was running over the allotted time and the meeting would probably run so late that he would not be able to see her that day.

"It was difficult for me to break away just to make this call," he explained, and then pleaded, "I hope you're not angry with me."

"Of course not," she assured him. "We'll get together another time. I'm actually glad things didn't work out for tonight. I'm awfully tired. I'll go for a little walk to get some fresh air, and then retire for the night."

"That doesn't sound very flattering," Richard chuckled. "I would have preferred for you to say that you miss me terribly and are counting the minutes until we can see each other again." There didn't seem to be anything that could dampen Richard's endless enthusiasm for life, and his jolly disposition.

"I miss you and will count the minutes until we see each other again," was Holly's quick retort. "I would think it a good idea, though, not to keep your client waiting any longer."

Richard laughed out loud and hung up the phone.

Holly always took the same path on her evening walks. First she went through the gardens, and then something invariably pulled her out to the fields -- to the place where she'd first met Michael. It seemed to her that an eternity had passed since that first meeting. How she wished things could have turned out differently. That Michael was only the field hand she'd first thought him to be. But so much had happened since that fateful day.

She still hadn't gotten over the shock of the senator's unexpected announcement of Michael's engagement to Margaret, and this on the same evening when he had declared his love to her, Holly. Something didn't seem right with such a sudden move. It never occurred to her that she, Holly, might be the cause of Michael's sudden decision to turn to Margaret.

The wedding was to take place in only four weeks. After that the couple would spend some time at the VanDorn Farm in Texas. Holly wasn't sure if she would be able to continue staying at the manor once they returned. Seeing Michael and Margaret together as man and wife might be too much for her to stomach. To see them day after day as a married couple would be unbearable.

Still deep in thought and puzzled over the sudden turn of events, Holly turned to retrace her steps and found herself unexpectedly face to face with Michael. The two young people stood there for a few moments, looking at each other in silence. Both were at a loss for words.

At last, Holly, not able to look at him any longer, gave a quick nod in his direction, and then attempted to continue her walk back to the manor. Michael's husky voice held her back.

"I love you." He didn't touch her -- just stood there, his arms hanging at his sides. But he said the three words in such a way that Holly felt them deep inside of herself.

She gave no sign of what she, herself, was feeling. She knew if she would give into her feelings, she would break down.

"It seems like you got over me quickly enough," she said instead, her voice filled with bitterness.

"Margaret knows that I don't love her," Michael answered quietly, but Holly could see the despair in his eyes.

"Look at me, Holly," he whispered hoarsely. "Look me in the eyes and tell me one more time that you don't love me. I will never bother you again if you can do that."

Holly did look into his eyes, opened her mouth... and couldn't get the words out.

"Why, Holly?" the young man had to ask in desperation. He still didn't dare touch her, fearing that she might run away. "There must be a reason why, from one moment to the next, you suddenly want nothing to do with me. You pushed me away twice, as a matter of fact."

Holly was no longer able to hold back. Tears streamed from her eyes and ran down her cheeks, and her entire body trembled. Now Michael did take her in his arms.

"Please don't cry," he begged, "but do tell me, please, what you imagine is standing between us."

"There is a possibility that you are my brother," Holly managed to get out between hiccups. "Or, at least, my half-brother."

Michael stiffened, stepped back to be able to look into her eyes, but refused to let go of her. At last he circled her face with his hands.

"What in the world makes you think so?" he asked, unable to comprehend what she had just said.

Holly took a deep breath, wiped the trailing tears off her face with the sleeve of her blouse, and then told him everything she'd learned since her mother's death. About the papers she'd found among her mother's other documents. About being adopted by the man she had believed to be her birth father. And about the leads she'd found that pointed to Seven Oaks.

"That's why I came here and took the job." Holly explained between more hiccups. "I was attempting to learn the truth of my birth, and at first I was new and thought I should learn my job, and then your father got sick and I certainly didn't want to bother him when he felt so badly."

Michael led her to a nearby bench. He cupped her chin in his hand and looked at the young woman thoughtfully. "My mother had already been dead for some time before you were born," he explained to Holly, "so there would have been no reason for my father to be secretive about a new love. Let me tell you a story," he continued, "and then you will realize why it is hard for me to believe that my father would have had an affair with another woman after my mother's death.

"As you might have heard, my father loved my mother very much. I think I have inherited that from him, the capacity of feeling very deeply when I care for someone. Although I must admit, I had never had those feeling before I met you. I do know that feelings in my family go deep and we do not turn to others quickly." He waved Holly off when she attempted to say something, assuming it concerned his pending marriage to Margaret.

"That thing I did with Margaret I did in desperation. I was half out of my mind when you turned me down once again and it appeared so final. Margaret took advantage of me when I was desperate. I don't think I would have married her, had it actually come down to it."

He seemed to gather his thoughts before he

continued. "My father blamed himself for my mother's death, which made it doubly hard for him to get over his loss. You probably noticed that, even though the manor is called Seven Oaks, there are only six of the big old trees standing around the pond in front."

"I meant to ask about that when I first arrived," Holly interrupted, "but with one thing and another happening, I never got around to it."

"Well, there's a reason for that," Michael continued his explanation. "One night, when my father was away on business, we had a severe thunderstorm. All the lights in the manor went out because of it, although the phone was still working. When it rang, my mother, who was frightened by the storm, rushed to answer it, thinking it might be my father. In her hurry, she fell in the dark, presumably stumbling over a piece of furniture and was seriously hurt. The cook called an ambulance, but before it could arrive, she heard a loud crash and discovered that one of the oaks had been hit by lightning and had crashed to the ground, blocking the driveway. By the time the EMTs could clear the way, my mother had died."

Michael looked up at Holly, tears in his eyes. Holly was crying again as well. Although neither knew Mrs. VanDorn -- Michael had been too young to remember her -- both felt the pain Drew VanDorn must have suffered when he arrived home to the horrifying news of his wife's death.

"My father never forgave himself for not having been there. He thinks to this day that he could have saved my mother. And he never replaced the tree." Michael took a deep breath. "The reason I'm telling you all this is to make you understand that my father would never have had an affair back then, because he loved my mother too much. I don't think he's seen another woman romantically at any time since."

"Perhaps you're right," Holly pondered what Michael had told her, "but why did he send my mother money for the first two years of my life, until I was adopted? There has to be a reason for that. I need to find out what it's all about. And I need to know who my birth father is. I have a feeling that, even if your father is not the one, he knows who it is."

Michael reached for her hands.

"We will talk to him together. I'm sure everything can be explained logically, and after we have heard that explanation, it will be possible for us to be happy together."

Their eyes met. Michael bent his head toward Holly's and touched her lips fleetingly with his. At the last minute he pulled back, but not before Holly had pushed with both of her hands against his chest.

"Don't," she said quietly.

Michael nodded his head in agreement. "We'll wait until we know. Now that I know what's been bothering you all this time, and that there is hope for us to be together after all, I can wait a while longer -- but not too long." He reached for her hand and they walked back to the manor house together. Michael was determined to talk to his father immediately. But he wouldn't get that chance.

Chapter 21

Gertrude came running toward them. The woman who was normally so composed and calm was nearly hysterical.

"You better hurry," she sobbed. "Your father..." She couldn't continue and started to sob harder, wiping her eyes with a dainty, lace-edged hanky.

Michael didn't waste any time. A few long strides brought him close to the housekeeper. He grabbed the woman's shoulder and shook her.

"What's wrong with him!?" he shouted at her, and without giving her a chance to say anything, "Damn it, tell me!"

Gertrude looked at him wide-eyed. Michael had never talked to her in this tone or manhandled her in such a manner. However, the shock of his actions did enable her to pull herself together enough to report the bad news to him, as they entered the living room.

"He had another heart attack," she managed to get out. "Dr. Ehmke is with him right now and he insists that we wait down here." Her handkerchief thoroughly soaked by now, Gertrude tucked it in one sleeve and pulled a Kleenex out of the other one to dry her streaming eyes. It did little good since she continued sobbing.

Michael didn't care what Dr. Ehmke had said. He wanted to be with his father -- to see him -- to make sure he was still alive. Holly stepped next to him and held onto his arm.

"Please Michael," she soothed. "I'm sure Dr. Ehmke will do everything he can and if you go up there, you will just get in the way and keep him from doing his job."

Michael had to agree that what Holly had said made sense. He forced himself to stay downstairs with the two women, but could not sit still. He paced up and down from one end of the room to the other.

The patience of the three anxious people was sorely tested as they waited for news of the senator's condition. Once or twice Michael made an attempt to go upstairs to see what was happening, but Holly managed to talk him out of it each time. At last three men slowly descended the stairs, two of them carrying a stretcher on which the senator's still, unconscious form was reclining. His breathing was labored, despite the oxygen mask that covered most of his face, a face that looked gray and sunken. The third man held an IV bag up high to allow its contents to drip into the patient's vein.

The doctor approached Michael and the two women, his face serious.

"The news is not good," he said, as usual not bothering to beat around the bush. He saw no need to cushion the blow since everyone here was aware of the senator's heart condition. Dr. Ehmke knew that they had expected something like this to happen, even if they had hoped that it wouldn't, at least not this soon.

Immediately, upon hearing the news, Gertrude started to sob even louder than before. Holly, who herself was shaking all over, nevertheless made an attempt to console the housekeeper, but it was in vain. The young woman could not help but worry about the senator, a man who had treated her much better than employers normally treat their employees. And she was so concerned about Michael. This man, who was so deathly ill, was, after all, his father.

"I'm going to the hospital." Michael's voice left no doubt that his mind was made up. He could not be talked out of this even though Dr. Ehmke told him to stay home, that there was nothing he could do for his father right now. The doctor explained to him that he would not be allowed to be with the senator, but instead, would have to wait in

A Mother's Sins

one of the waiting rooms. Michael didn't care. All he wanted was to be as near his father as he possibly could.

"I'll go with you," Holly assured Michael. She noticed Dr. Ehmke's strange look. Then she remembered that he'd been one of the guests at the Harvest Festival and knew about Michael's engagement to Margaret. But, Holly thought, this is not the time for explanations. Let him think what he wants. We can tell him our story later on, at a more appropriate time.

The doctor rushed to the ambulance where the men were busy getting the senator ready for the trip to the hospital. One of them gave a slight shake of the head when the doctor approached him and asked a question so quietly, that Holly could not make it out.

She seemed to have been the only one to notice the quick gesture, and she didn't assume that it was an indication of anything good; instead she feared and expected the worst.

Michael wanted to follow the ambulance in his car, but Holly who'd calmed down a little, took the keys from him.

"I don't think you're in any shape to be driving right now," she said.

Michael didn't argue with her. "I'm glad you're here with me," was all he said.

"I like your father," she told him, "and perhaps..." she stopped for a moment, "perhaps he is also my father."

Not one of them had remembered that Margaret was somewhere in the house and should be given the news. Consequently, she knew nothing about the senator's heart attack. But they all new that this cold and calculating woman would not let the state of health of the man she still thought of as her future father-in-law bother her. She had more important things to worry about, as far as she was concerned. She would not give it a rest until she had Michael's diamond on her ring finger and the wedding license safely in her hand.

Holly ignored all traffic rules as she was driving Michael to the hospital. She decided the best course would be to stay close behind the ambulance, which was racing along, lights flashing, and sirens screaming.

While the doctors fought for Drew VanDorn's life, Holly and Michael paced back and forth in the small waiting room at the end of the hall. The waiting was nerve wracking, and they could not bring themselves to sit down, here any more than at home, although there Michael had been the only one to pace. Holly had been too busy trying to calm Mrs. Walters down.

Around midnight Dr. Ehmke approached the two young people. His look told them that the senator's condition had not improved.

"If you like," he told Michael, "you can visit your father for a moment.

Michael, who had finally been persuaded by Holly moments ago to take a seat, jumped up immediately, trying to pull her with him. Dr. Ehmke stopped him. "Actually I shouldn't let even you into the room." He looked at Holly. "I hope you understand."

Holly nodded her head and squeezed Michael's hand. "Go ahead, I'll wait here."

Dr. Ehmke stayed with Holly as Michael disappeared from view through the swinging doors a nurse held open for him. She was there to help him dress in sterile clothes.

When Michael could no longer be seen, the doctor turned to Holly. "I know this isn't the right time, and, it's actually not my business, but I can sense that there is something between you and the senator's son.

"Oh, doctor," Holly sighed, "It's all much too complicated to explain right now. We will explain it to you when things have settled down a bit."

He didn't say anything more since it was, indeed, none of his business, but he thought to himself that he much preferred for Michael to marry this young woman than the one he had gotten himself engaged to. For some

A Mother's Sins

reason he had developed an intense dislike for Margaret. He now asked Holly, "Could I have a nurse bring you some coffee or anything else?"

Holly shook her head, but then changed her mind.

"A cup of coffee would be nice. I have a feeling this will be a long night for us."

The doctor left soon after, but promised to return later to keep her informed about the senator's condition.

Half an hour later, Michael returned.

"He's doing a little better," he told Holly and there was some hope in his voice. "The doctors are confident that, if he'll make it through the night, he'll recover."

He pulled her into his arms for a brief moment.

"You look exhausted," he said. "Why don't you drive on home?"

Holly shook her head.

"I will stay with you as long as necessary," she told him firmly. "But we should call Gertrude. I'm sure she's terribly worried."

Michael made the call. He was glad to have something to do, something that would occupy his mind for a while. As Holly had predicted, Gertrude had been frantic not knowing how the senator was doing. She had been sitting next to the phone the entire time, waiting for news. Since she did not drive, she'd actually been about ready to walk to the hospital to see how her employer was doing. Now she breathed a sigh of relief when Michael brought her up to date. But they all knew that the danger was far from over, that there would be a few more hours of worry in store for them.

Two hours later, Michael was, once more, allowed to visit his father for a few minutes. The senator was sleeping deeply, and the prospect of his recovery grew with each passing hour.

When daylight made its first appearance, Holly and Michael considered driving home, but Dr. Ehmke who came, once more, into the small waiting room stopped them. He looked very tired and his face was grim.

"I bring bad news," he said, brushing a hand over his eyes. "It seems that the senator was feeling much worse during the last few weeks than he let us know."

Michael's face turned ashen. "Are you telling us...?" He broke off, unable to finish the sentence -- to voice the awful possibility.

The doctor nodded. "We weren't able to do any more for your father. His heart gave out and he went quietly in his sleep. I do hope it will make you feel a little better to know that he did not suffer."

Chapter 22

For the first time Margaret showed Michael her true face, "Does that mean that we will not be able to marry when we had planned?" She had the gall to ask.

Holly was unable to hide the distaste she felt after hearing the other woman's words. Michael was speechless. He couldn't believe this woman whom he'd asked to be his wife could be so callous. It was Gertrude who finally found the words to tell Margaret in no uncertain terms just what they all thought of her.

"Of all the nerve! Senator VanDorn hasn't been dead for twenty-four hours yet and the only thing you whine about is whether your wedding will take place as planned."

"None of that is any of your business," true to her usual self, Margaret was looking down her nose at Gertrude, the lowly housekeeper, the servant, just as she did with everyone she considered inferior to her, and she didn't hesitate to let her know it, no matter the situation. Her "I'm better than you" attitude irritated Holly who, nevertheless, kept quiet. Trying to convince this woman how insensitive she was would be useless. Margaret would never change. The redhead, however, wasn't finished. "I have no intentions of discussing my private affairs with you. Servants should be seen, not heard," she paraphrased.

Ever since Margaret had learned of the senator's death, she had started to consider herself mistress of Seven Oaks. The fact that Michael had lost his father left her cold. With her warped thought processes, the situation had actually turned for the better as far as she was concerned. Michael was now the heir to a considerate fortune, and as his wife, she planned to tell him how to spend it. It was so much more important, she felt, to be the actual mistress of the manor instead of being tagged as the senator's daughter-in-law.

At first she had pretended that she cared about Michael's loss, until he'd talked about postponing their wedding indefinitely. Her whole body had trembled, mostly from anger, when he'd mentioned this. She'd already disliked the fact that the simple secretary had spent the entire night with Michael at the hospital -- and now this. Not that Margaret would have stayed around for any length of time or been any help to Michael, had she been the one to accompany him in the first place. But that had been something else that had stuck in her craw. Nobody had bothered to tell her about the senator's collapse. She hadn't even known that he had a bad heart. But she was mostly angry because it was evident that, ever since that night, Michael and the girl seemed to have become quite intimate.

"Why don't you say something," she now shouted at Michael, who felt as though he were seeing the young woman for the very first time. It was almost as though he'd been wearing blinders when he'd run into her again down there in Texas after all those years, and now those blinders had been taken off. He asked himself how he could ever have considered spending the rest of his life with this person. It seemed as though his father had done him a final favor through his death; he had made him see what manner of person Margaret O'Mally really was.

At the moment, however, Michael was not in any shape to argue with the woman. His feelings were all mixed up. He was tired, and upset, and sad. He wanted to be alone with Holly and forget that Margaret even existed. His face clearly showed the pain he was experiencing at the loss of his father, but his almost-to-be wife didn't have a clue how he felt, nor did she care.

"We'll talk about it later," Michael managed to get

out as he looked at Margaret. "Right now I have other things to think about."

The woman, however, was not one with the inclination to wait when she wanted something. She attempted to argue with Michael, to tell him that she had a right to know where she stood in this. But one look from him was enough to silence her at last. It was evident that she didn't want to ruin any chance she might still have to marry the heir to Seven Oaks and all that went with it. Nothing else would have kept her still at this point.

In the afternoon, Willard Graham made his not unexpected appearance. He was grief-stricken at the loss of his friend and looked years older.

"Michael," Graham put his arms around the younger man. "I don't know what to say. It all came so suddenly. I simply can't believe he is gone."

"I feel the same way," Michael sighed. "I don't think it has completely sunk in yet, and yes, it seems so unexpected. That is, of course, because he didn't tell any of us how sick he actually was."

"I should have noticed it on my last visit, though. He did look quite ill then, but I assumed it was because he was just recuperating from the other attack." Graham tried to take some of the blame for his friend's death.

"Nonsense," Gertrude would have none of it. As much as she suffered from her employer's sudden death, she would not let his kindly old friend blame himself for what had been inevitable. "We all know how stubborn the senator was. None of us would have been able to prevent his death."

Graham now noticed Holly who had been sitting quietly in an armchair, her face pale, her eyes staring through the window, but seemingly looking at nothing. She rose when she heard the senator's friend call her name. As she turned her head, he again had the feeling that he should know this young woman. He was convinced that he'd met her somewhere before. But it was no use;

hard as he tried, he couldn't remember. He'd been thinking about her quite a lot since the last time he'd seen her, but had been unable to place her.

He walked toward her now and held out his hand. "I certainly had not expected to greet you so soon again and certainly not under these circumstances," he told her taking both of her hands in his and looking at her closely.

Holly was glad that Graham had come to be with Michael. She didn't know what was going through his mind, but had taken a liking to the older man who was always friendly and warm toward her although he barely knew her. She sensed instinctively that, if there was one human being who could give Michael the emotional support he needed right now, this was the one. He and the senator had been very close, so it should be easy for Michael to talk about his father to what had been the latter's good friend, should he feel the need to do so.

Gertrude had left to see to dinner, and Holly thought it might be a good idea to leave as well to give the men a chance to talk, and to see if Gertrude could use a hand, but neither would allow her to leave.

"Please stay," Michael pleaded, and when Willard Graham reached for her hand and smiled at her in his friendly manner, then insisted as well that she stay, she allowed herself to be persuaded and sat back down.

"I don't want to stick my nose into your business," Graham told Michael. "But if you need any help, you only have to ask."

Michael nodded gratefully. One of the things that had been bothering him was the thought of having to arrange for his father's funeral.

"I'm sure you'll understand that I feel I should take care of that myself," he tried to explain to Graham. "I owe my father that much. But it would help me a lot if I could ask for your advice now and then."

Graham decided that, if he was going to help these young people, it would be best if he spent the next few days, at least until the funeral, at Seven Oaks. He wanted

A Mother's Sins

to be on hand should Michael need him, and he wanted to be able to advise him in the multiple tasks that awaited the younger man's attention when the funeral was over.

After he'd left the room to get some much needed rest in one of the guestrooms, Michael and Holly found themselves alone for the first time since leaving the hospital.

Michael sat down on the armrest of Holly's chair and placed his arm around her shoulders.

"I'm so glad to have you with me," he said quietly. "Whether you are my sister or not, I don't know how I would have made it through the last few hours without you."

"I'm so terribly sad about the death of your father," Holly could barely get the words out. Her voice was raspy, and her throat seemed to be so tight it felt almost closed. Tears were very close to the surface. "He was such a good man and treated me almost like a daughter, although he had no idea that I actually might be." She leaned her head against Michael, unable to hold the tears back any longer.

There was one subject Holly and Michael both had on their mind, but it was something they had not yet discussed, didn't really want to discuss at present. They were very much aware that, with the senator's death, there was now no one left who could tell them with certainty whether they were or were not brother and sister.

Ursula Turner

Chapter 23

The day of the senator's funeral dawned gray and dreary. How could it be otherwise, Holly thought. It fit right in with the mood of the small group of people who accompanied the senator to his last resting-place. Michael had been aware that his father had wanted only family and close friends to attend his burial and had seen to it that the news of the senator's death had not appeared in any of the newspapers. Later on, it would have to be publicized, since he had been a well-known and well-liked political figure.

Michael VanDorn walked behind the coffin, which was being carried by some of the field workers from the small chapel to the family cemetery. He looked neither right nor left and appeared numb with grief; however, through his sorrow, he was aware that Margaret was walking next to him as though she belonged there. And it felt wrong.

Holly should be walking by his side instead, he thought, but this was not the time to go into that, he decided. It was clear, however, that he would have to have a talk with this obstinate woman as soon as possible. He would have to inform her that he was not able -- no -- that he did not want to marry her. He would explain to her that there was absolutely no love between them and that they would only succeed in making each other miserable through the years. He would tell her that he'd buy her ranch, and that he'd give her more money than it was worth. If necessary, he would even offer to pay off her debts if they weren't too exorbitant. That was really all that the greedy Texan was after anyway, and he hoped this generosity would buy her off -- would get rid of her once and for all.

Immediately after the funeral, some of the mourners, the ones Richard Storm had notified earlier, gathered in the library where the attorney read the senator's will. Drew VanDorn must have sensed that the time he had left on earth was running out. He had changed his will only a few days before his death.

Willard Graham received a collection of books; old volumes that the senator had known his friend would treasure. None of the field hands, nor the domestic help, had been forgotten, each receiving a small monetary award. He had remembered Gertrude Walters in a special way. The housekeeper sobbed out loud when she heard that her employer had given her the right to remain as resident of the manor for the rest of her life, with an added pension that would allow her to live independently.

Holly reached for Gertrude's hand and leaned toward her, "He liked you very much," she tried to console the older woman, although she knew from experience that there was nothing she or anybody else could say or do to lessen the housekeeper's grief. Holly was aware that she was the only one who realized that Gertrude had been in love with the senator. She also knew that the old saying was true, that time heals all wounds.

The young woman was surprised to learn that the senator had remembered her as well and had left her a sizable sum of money. When Richard read the amount, Margaret's eyes blazed. The redhead had received no invitation from the lawyer, but had chosen to attend the meeting anyway. Since Michael had not had the opportunity to speak to her in private about his future plans, she was still under the mistaken impression that she had a right to be there, and the young heir had not wanted to have a confrontation at this particular time. At any rate, Drew VanDorn had left her absolutely nothing, even though his changing his will had occurred after she and Michael had become engaged and she had been expected to become part of the family.

Later that afternoon, Michael and Willard Graham met in the senator's office. Graham could tell that Michael felt uncomfortable sitting at his father's old desk. It was evident that he wasn't as yet ready to take over the reins. Although he wasn't interested in politics and had no plans to seek public office, he would be taking over the management of all his father's businesses and properties, which were considerable.

"It'll take time, my boy," Graham tried to reassure Michael. "But we do need to talk before I leave tomorrow."

Michael nodded his head, indicating that he was ready to listen to his father's old friend. But first he went to the sideboard and reached for a bottle and two glasses, then poured each of them about two fingers of bourbon. He carried the glasses to the desk, handed one to Graham, and sat back down.

"Are you still planning to buy Margaret O'Mally's ranch?" Graham asked after he'd taken a small sip of the amber liquid.

"I didn't have a lot of time to discuss the entire deal with father," Michael explained. "The thing that was of the most interest to both of us was the horses, and I don't suppose we would have to buy the ranch to get them. However, I've been doing a lot of thinking lately, and I have changed my mind about marrying Margaret. She caught me at a bad time, and I proposed to her in desperation. But since then I've had a lot of time to consider the implications of marrying this very cold woman, and I have come to the conclusion that we simply are not compatible. I had a reason for asking her to marry me, but that reason no longer exists. Besides, I think she wanted me for my money, or actually father's, and has no conception of what true love is. Money, of course, is not a good basis to build a life on, don't you agree?" Michael took a deep breath so he could tell the rest as quickly as possible. "I have decided to buy her ranch. If necessary I will pay more for it than it is worth, as long as that will get rid of her."

A Mother's Sins

"Hold your horses, there," Graham held up both hands as though that would stop Michael's deluge of words, although the young man seemed to be all talked out anyway. Graham had breathed a deep sigh of relief after hearing about Michael's change of plans concerning the marriage. However, he did not want to see the young man get in over his head when it came to buying Margaret's ranch. "I would advise against that purchase," he therefore now said. "I've been able to learn that, should you buy the ranch, some of the debt would transfer to you. You would lose so much through this transaction that it would take years to recoup the losses."

Michael stared at his father's portrait, on the opposite wall. He chewed on his lower lip while thinking about what Graham had told him.

"I know, of course, that you are engaged to Margaret. I also know that your father strongly disapproved of the woman," Graham continued. "However, I wonder if you should have to go to such extremes to call off the engagement. In any case, I would advise caution. Talk to the woman first before you commit yourself to anything."

Michael rose and walked to a window that looked out on the gardens, but had no idea what he was looking at.

"You don't know Margaret O'Mally," he finally said in response to the older man's advice. "I believe that she is a very vindictive woman. She would not hesitate to sue me for breech of promise. She has plenty of witnesses that I did, indeed, propose to her, or, at least, that I did not object when my father made the announcement. She would do anything to get her hands on some money. But no matter what the consequences are -- I can't marry her. The two of us have absolutely nothing in common and, more recently, since my father's death actually, I have come to despise her. She is a person with no feelings for others. She considers only her own to be of any importance. Yet, I still feel that I have to make it up to her somehow that I've decided not to marry her."

"That's an honorable thought," Graham was impressed. "Perhaps you could check out her ranch further. If possible, you might buy a small portion of the land along with her remaining horses, especially since you seem to be interested in them more than in any of Margaret's other property."

"Not a bad idea," Michael was thinking out loud now. "Margaret's horses are supposed to be quite valuable. Father had her checked out after she came to the manor and learned that an old man, the only person to still work for her, has been taking excellent care of the animals, and that he is particularly good with horses. Perhaps I'll be able to hire him if I decide to buy them. From what I've heard, he hasn't been paid his wages for several months and is only staying on because of his love for the animals and also because he has no other place to stay." Michael looked up when he realized he'd been rambling, again, but he had to finish his train of thought. "First, of course, I'll have to discuss the whole business with Margaret as you suggested, and then I'll still need your advice when it comes to the actual purchase."

"I'll be glad to help in any way I can. You know that," Graham assured the younger man. He stood up and started to leave, but there was something he'd been wondering about, something that had been bothering him, and he decided he might as well ask.

"May I inquire what your main reason was that you lost your interest in marrying Margaret O'Mally? I know you said you didn't feel you two were compatible, but I sense that there is something else, another, much stronger reason for you to break up with the young woman."

Michael turned his head briefly to look at Graham, and then stared out at the gardens again. He'd known that Graham hadn't totally accepted his explanation for the break-up. He decided to tell him the truth.

"Margaret doesn't happen to be the woman I love."

"The way you say that leads me to believe that

A Mother's Sins

there is another woman in the picture. Let me guess," he continued, with a small smile playing at the corners of his mouth. "You wouldn't be in love with Holly Snyder?"

When Michael nodded his head, Graham stepped closer and put his arm around his shoulders.

"A smart choice," he praised, "with which your father would certainly have been happy. That young lady is a perfect match for you as far as I can see."

"That might be," Michael's eyes were downcast now as he tried to explain their problem to his father's friend. "Holly and I can never plan on a future together. You see, there is a good possibility that she is my sister."

Graham was thunderstruck. He looked at the young man as though he had lost his mind. Then, as soon as he had pulled himself together, he insisted that Michael tell him the whole story.

Michael was only too glad to be given the chance of sharing his problems with someone he knew he could trust. He told Willard Graham everything exactly the way Holly had told it to him.

Graham looked quite thoughtful when he, finally, left the late senator's office.

Chapter 24

Margaret was pacing her room. In her anger she moved faster and faster, from the window to the door, and back. She was furious about the way Michael and Holly seemed to be drawn to each other, were spending more and more time together while, at the same time, Michael was very obviously avoiding Margaret. He had some nerve, she thought. Did he not realize how he was hurting her feelings? As usual, the young woman thought only of herself, and she made up her mind that she would not put up with the way he was treating her, his future wife, much longer. She was determined to put an end to his time with Holly.

She had already made one attempt to talk to Michael about the situation. But her so-called fiancé had come up with several, in her opinion, lame excuses about how busy he was right now while he was trying to get a grip on running his father's various businesses. He'd also tried to explain to her that, since he'd never had sole responsibility for this, he had to spend a lot of time with all of it while trying to learn the ropes. She wasn't as stupid as he thought she was, though. She knew that he was only saying that to keep from having to explain why he was ignoring her so much lately, as well as his recent shabby treatment of her.

She was actually losing some sleep over the fact that he was no longer mentioning anything about their getting married, hadn't even as much as talked about setting a new date. She had an ominous feeling about that secretary, who had the audacity to think she was an equal to Margaret and Michael. Margaret also knew that the other woman was to blame for Michael's sudden distance to her, his fiancée. They had better not try to put one over on her by saying that Michael needed her to do secretarial work for him. In Margaret's opinion this woman no longer had any business at the manor. After all, the senator was dead, and therefore her job no longer existed. And Michael might as well get used to the idea that as long as she, Margaret, was around, he'd better be hiring an old, gray-haired woman to take care of the office work.

Margaret still remembered vividly the night she'd seen Michael profess his love to the other woman and how he had been turned away by her. She was almost sure she'd come up with a reason for Holly's earlier behavior toward Michael. It was clear that the woman had made plans to marry the senator because, if and when she became his widow, she'd inherit a bundle. However, since the senator had died before she could latch onto him, she had picked Michael as her next victim. Being married to somebody rich was, at least in Margaret's eyes, almost as good as inheriting from somebody who had a lot of money.

With that thought in mind, Margaret was angry with herself that she hadn't thought of catching the senator for herself. All of her problems would have been taken care of. But as things stood, she had better get back to the situation with Michael and the other woman, and try to control his actions while she was still able to do something about it. Simply put, there was no way she would stand by and watch Holly take Michael away from her, not without a fight, she grimly told herself. She would claw and scratch for what she considered hers.

By now Margaret had worked herself into such a rage, she was unable to remain in her room a minute longer. She had to take some action now, this very moment. As it happened, the first person to cross her path was Holly, who was walking along the downstairs hallway.

"I think it's about time you started packing your bags," Margaret hissed at Holly, whom she now considered her rival despite her lowly standings as secretary and servant. Holly didn't know what this was all about but tried to stay calm.

"I don't think that's for you to decide," she told the angry redhead. "As long as Michael VanDorn needs me, I will stay at the manor."

"As long as he needs you?" Margaret threw her head back and laughed out loud. "I'm wise to you, my dear. But, since you couldn't get anywhere with the senator, what makes you think you'll succeed with his son?" Margaret's laughter sounded close to hysteria by now.

"You acted pretty stupid," she sneered, "You already had the little fish on the hook, but he wasn't big enough for you. So you threw him back to snare the big one. But it didn't work out for you, did it? The big one got away from you."

Holly stepped back. Her face had turned pale. She couldn't believe that Margaret could be so vicious as to accuse her of such thoughts and deeds, but the other woman wasn't done yet.

"Too bad death was faster than you. But I will not permit you to get your greedy claws into Michael, too. He is my fiancé, and don't you forget it!"

Since Holly had no idea how to respond to these dreadful, although unfounded accusations, she felt relieved when she realized she wouldn't have to. Michael who had heard everything Margaret had said to Holly as he was coming down the stairs had stopped on the last landing. He was just as bewildered about Margaret's attack on Holly as Holly herself had been. At the same time, he was terribly angry.

"Enough!" His command came loud and clear.

The redhead jumped, turned, saw Michael, and realized immediately that she'd gone too far. Yet, she wasn't in the least sorry for what she'd said to Holly, only for the fact that Michael had heard her say it. She was also annoyed at herself for not having been a little more careful. Now she tried to smooth things over, at least as much as was possible under the circumstances.

A Mother's Sins

Her eyes suddenly filled with tears.

"Michael," she sobbed. "I'm so glad you're here. I insist that you dismiss this woman immediately," she pointed her coral-tipped finger at Holly. "You can't imagine how she screamed at me and the names she called me, your future wife."

"I only heard what you said to Holly," he answered, keeping his voice under control, and descending the rest of the steps. He felt somewhat guilty for not having informed Margaret about his change of heart and that he would not be marrying her. There had been a time or two when he could have said something, but somehow couldn't get up the courage, knowing in advance how she would react.

Now Margaret ran toward him and started to throw herself into his arms. When she noticed the steely look in Michael's eyes, she stopped short.

"I got carried away," she tried to explain, lowering her eyes. "If you'd been here a few minutes earlier, you would have heard all the things she threw at me first."

Michael cast a swift glance in Holly's direction. She hadn't made a move or said a word during Margaret's accusations. He gave her a quick smile to let her know he hadn't fallen for Margaret's grandstand show.

"I hadn't planned to tell you in quite this way," Michael turned back toward Margaret. "I had hoped that during the next few days, after I had taken care of some of the more pressing business, we would be able to have a quiet conversation. But after the scene I just witnessed, you leave me no choice. I will not marry you, Margaret; therefore, our engagement is null and void. I don't love you, and I have come to the conclusion that we don't see things the same way and never will. Marriage would never work for us."

"You can't do that to me!" Margaret shrieked. She couldn't believe what she'd just heard. This had to be a bad dream. She ran toward Michael and clung to him. "You can't do that, Michael!" she repeated in desperation. "We're engaged; you gave me your word!"

"Margaret!" Michael tore himself lose. "Stop your play-acting. This is the twenty-first century. An engagement is only a test to see if a lifelong commitment between two people will work out. We did not pass this test, and we should leave it at that. In fact, we should be thankful that we found out in time and won't be making each other miserable for the rest of our lives."

Margaret had paid no attention to his words. She knew only that there was no changing Michael's mind -- that he would, under no circumstances, marry her now.

All of her plans of once again, being able to afford a life of luxury had fallen apart. All of her scheming had been in vain.

"You will pay for this," she looked at Michael, her eyes glittering with pure hate. Then she turned and saw Holly, who'd been watching the scene almost as though in a trance.

"There won't be a single day for either one of you to enjoy any happiness," Margaret spit at Holly. Her words sounded almost as though she were putting a curse on the two of them.

That same day Margaret O'Mally left Seven Oaks.

Holly, however, felt little relief. She could still hear the other woman's screeching voice and her threat, and she was convinced that Margaret was fully capable of following through on it, contrary to Michael, who was only too happy that he no longer had to put up with the woman's irritating presence. And he laughed at Holly's worries.

Even though Margaret's threat remained on Holly's mind and was something she continued to worry about, neither of the young people would admit to the other that the only thing that could destroy their happiness totally and completely would be to find out that they were brother and sister. And should that be the case, Margaret's threat could not, by the remotest stretch of their imagination, be considered worse.

Chapter 25

Holly and the young heir of Seven Oaks spent an entire day in the manor's archives, searching for any shred of information, any small mention that might tell them of a connection between the senator and Holly's mother. However, aside from the documents Holly had discovered on her earlier foray, they were unable to find anything new. There was nothing at all that could have told them why the senator had sent money to Holly's mother. If a love affair had, indeed, existed, Drew VanDorn had been extremely discreet about it.

"Being secretive like that just doesn't sound like something my father would do," Michael shook his head in despair. Miserable at not having found an answer to their dilemma and wondering what to do next, he thought out loud, "He would never have hidden the woman he loved. He was generally very open about everything he did."

Holly, who wanted very much to be in Michael's arms instead of looking through dusty stacks of old documents that did not tell them what they wanted to know, agreed with his conclusion. "I got to know your father fairly well during the short time I worked for him, and I must admit that I got the same impression. He was not a secretive man. I only wish I would have had the courage to come right out in the beginning and asked him about everything. But on the day I was finally brave enough to approach him with my questions, he got sick, and there was no way that I would have bothered him with my problem at that time. I reasoned that it might have been too painful for him to think back at that particular time of his life, and he certainly didn't need any added heartache while on his sickbed. But because of my cowardice I'm not sure we'll ever learn the truth about me and my ancestry now."

She started to replace the documents into the file drawers where they'd been kept for so many years.

"It might be best if I leave here as soon as possible," she couldn't bring herself to look at Michael as she voiced her thoughts.

"No, you can't do that to me!" Michael's response was quick. He reached for her, grasping her shoulders so hard that she winced and, while her back was turned to him, he took advantage and nuzzled her ear with his lips. "Holly, you mustn't leave me," he begged. "I can't stand another separation from you. The first one was hard enough, but to part again...," he didn't finish what she knew he wanted to say.

"I've thought about it at length," Holly hadn't moved an inch. Her voice was no more than a whisper. "It would be so much easier for both of us if we didn't see each other day after day. Receiving daily reminders that there can never be even as much as this for us is simply unbearable for me."

Michael couldn't and wouldn't listen to her. It was just as unbearable for him to think about her leaving the manor forever.

He let go of her and threw his hands up. "There has to be some way to find out the truth," he almost shouted, knocking a pile of neatly stacked papers to the floor out of sheer frustration.

Without a word, Holly bent down, picked them up and began to sort through them once more.

"Please forgive me," Michael laid his hand on her arm. "I should have better control of my temper, but this whole thing is so frustrating, and I can't bear the thought of you leaving here. Won't you reconsider? It would make me happy just to know you are near."

Holly shook her head, "You know as well as I do that, after a while, that sort of arrangement wouldn't be enough for either one of us. As much as I feel drawn to you -- and each day more so -- it would not be sufficient for me just to be in your company. One day we'd both become desperate and give in to our desires, and afterward we'd feel guilty. And we'd begin to hate each other because of those guilt feelings. That's something I don't want to take a chance of ever happening."

Michael drew her into his arms. It felt so natural to him to have her there; it was as though she belonged there. He was touched by the way she snuggled against him, trusting him not to do anything he shouldn't. He inhaled the aroma of her cologne for an instant, then forced himself to speak, "You're right, of course, and evidently also the smarter one of the two of us," he admitted quietly, hugging her even closer, then gently pushed her away. How could he suppress his boundless love for her? He wanted her to feel protected by him, and not as though she were forced to run away from him, as she was practically planning to do. But what other choice was there? Until they knew something definite, they had to regard themselves as brother and sister.

"It will be very hard for me to leave here," Holly's voice was hoarse from unshed tears, and her throat felt closed, "just as hard as it is for you to let me go. But I've already made the arrangements since I didn't really expect to find anything new among these papers. I will return to my hometown, find an apartment there and get a job. People know me there and it shouldn't be too difficult to find employment. It had also entered my mind that, the quicker I left, the easier it would be."

Michael bit his lip until he tasted blood. He wanted to scream, but had to agree with Holly. She was doing the right thing.

"Will we see each other again?" was all he could think to say.

Holly shook her head, "Probably not," she answered him. "I love you Michael, but in spite of that, or perhaps because of it, I wish we had never met."

Despite the heartache, Holly felt better after having told Michael what she planned to do. It was a relief to get that much off her chest. Of course, it didn't ease her overall troubles. Although there'd been no real reason to expect anything more, she had felt just a tiny speck of anticipation, a little spark of hope that made her believe there was a possibility that they might find something in the senator's papers after all, something that would shed some light on her ancestry, something that might have helped the two of them in some way. However, sadly, in spite of their anticipation, there had been nothing.

"I would have preferred to have found proof that you are indeed my sister, rather than to be left in limbo like this," Michael must have been following the same train of thought. "This uncertainty is so much harder to take. I can't help but think about how happy we could be if we only knew..."

He looked into Holly's tear-filled eyes. "Aren't you sometimes angry with your mother for not having told you the truth -- for causing you to find out only part of the facts the way you did, and then leaving you to wonder about the rest?"

Holly considered his question carefully for a long moment, then shook her head.

"We have no right to judge the actions of our parents," was her comment. "I am sad because she never told me about my real father -- didn't even let me know that I'd been adopted by the man I'd considered to be my dad. But I'm certain she thought she was doing the right thing. There was no way for her to know how much pain and suffering her silence would cause."

Michael drew Holly into his arms one more time, realizing it would probably be the last time for them to be this close. He couldn't understand why Holly was suddenly in such a hurry to leave Seven Oaks and him. There were so many things he hadn't had a chance to share with her. He wanted to be able to feast his eyes on her, and since that would not be possible much longer, he wanted to memorize her every feature. He even suggested that he would take care of her financially, at least until she'd be able to find a job. He was, in a way, trying anything and everything to make it possible for them to stay in touch.

Holly had been aware of the problem between them much longer than he and, consequently, had become more adjusted to the idea. Since Michael had just learned about their circumstances a few days ago, it was much more difficult for him to accept the fact that they had to part.

"It'll be better if we break off any relationship between us completely," she now suggested, then turned and rushed up the stairs and toward her rooms before he could see her burst into tears, making everything even more difficult for him. She couldn't bear to see the sorrow in his eyes.

But there was no possibility for her to run away from her own pain.

Chapter 26

While Holly was in the process of loading her suitcase into the trunk of her little, old car, which had been repaired some time ago and was now in perfect running order, a limousine pulled up next to her at the bottom of the wide staircase.

Willard Graham jumped out of the vehicle evidently in a great hurry since he hadn't given his chauffeur a chance to open the door for him.

"You're leaving?" Graham asked, reaching for Holly's hand.

She nodded, unable to get out the words. Her face was pale and her eyes were red from crying. But she had cried herself out and was determined not to shed any more tears. She felt she had to be strong now. She owed that much to Michael, who was, just then, coming down the steps.

"I must speak with you," Graham told Holly, and there was suppressed excitement in his voice. "And this will interest you, too," he turned to Michael. "Thank God I got here in time."

Neither Michael nor Holly could imagine why Graham was so excited, but they, obediently, followed him inside, where he led them to the small sitting room.

After closing the door, Graham stood there for a moment, looking at the two young people who looked back at him expectantly. At last he took a deep breath, walked toward Holly, and reached for her hand. This time he began to talk without beating around the bush.

"Before you leave here, you should know that I am...," here he hesitated as though he was having difficulties with what he was about to say. But he quickly continued, "...that I am your father," he finished the sentence, then held his breath in anticipation of how the two young people would react to his announcement.

For a moment it was deathly still in the room. Holly stared at Graham, the man who had just informed her that he was the father she'd come here to find, in disbelief. How could this be? Had she heard correctly? She must be dreaming and would wake up shortly -- in her old room in her mother's house.

"What did you say?" It was no dream. She recognized Michael's voice, even though it sounded hoarse. He must be feeling the same way she did.

"I am Holly's father!" Graham looked from one young face to the other, trying to read their true reactions to his news, trying to gage how they felt about his sudden disclosure. However, they were still far too bewildered to show any kind of reaction other than shock.

"You must believe me, Holly. I loved your mother with all my heart," Graham tried to assure her.

"But why? What happened?"

"Why did I leave her? Why did I not acknowledge our child?"

Holly nodded.

Graham placed his arm around her shoulders and led her to a chair near the window. He wanted to be able to study her face as he told his story.

Holly was glad to sit. What she had just heard had come as quite a shock and, although her knees felt like they were made of rubber, she was only now aware how tense the rest of her had been since the older man's announcement.

She had to admit to herself that, so far she was not yet able to regard this man as her father. Although she had liked him very much from the start, and there had been a feeling of familiarity every time she saw him, he remained Graham for the time being, even in her thoughts. She looked at the man, still not convinced she'd heard correctly. She wasn't convinced yet that the whole thing wasn't a dream after all.

But in the next instant, as she studied Graham as he was talking to her, she knew this was reality, because she began to realize why Graham had seemed so familiar when she'd first seen him. It was the resemblance between them. She had inherited his eyes, as well as some of his other features, including the way her lips curved when she smiled.

Suddenly, she couldn't help but put on that smile. Willard Graham was her father! She was suddenly quite certain of the fact, even before he'd told her the entire story, which he was about to do.

"When I fell in love with your mother, I was still married," her father had decided it would be best to bare his soul and tell all. "I know I did not behave honorably at that time."

Glancing at the far wall for an instant, he appeared to be ashamed of his past actions and he seemed to try to avoid any kind of eye contact with his daughter for that moment.

But he continued quickly, "I fought against my feelings, as did your mother. My wife was very ill at the time. That's why I couldn't bring myself to leave her. Your mother understood. We separated and buried our love deep inside. But then I learned she was with child. My child!"

Graham stopped again. It seemed painful for him to relive those days. "Thinking it over long and hard," he continued, "I decided to acknowledge both your mother and you. But she wouldn't hear of it. She felt sorry for my wife, even though she didn't know her. Your mother was a loving and kind woman."

"I know," Holly's voice was low. "She could never have managed to hurt anyone deliberately."

"That's right," it was Graham's turn again. "She insisted that we not see each other any more. She said that she had gotten the better deal, that she had proof of

A Mother's Sins

our love -- you -- while I had nothing."

Now Graham felt compelled to sit down, too. He chose a chair next to Holly. Her face had already told him that she was not at all upset with him and nor was she judging him for his actions. She was a lot like her mother, he thought.

"Your mother didn't even want me to help her financially with the baby. She was worried that my wife, who was deathly ill by then, would find out. That's why I asked my friend Drew to send your mother the checks. He was the only person who knew my story. And that's how his name came to be on the papers you found."

"That's why all indications pointed to Seven Oaks," Holly whispered.

Graham nodded. "Then, after the first two years, all the checks that Drew was sending were returned with the envelopes unopened. Your mother had moved without leaving a forwarding address. Both Drew and I tried to find her which was, as I now realize, futile, since we didn't know at the time that she had changed her name as well as her address."

"Yes," Holly acknowledged, "She married Bill Snyder, the man who I thought was my father."

"Did he treat you well?" Graham had to know.

"He never let me know in any way that I was not his child," Holly assured him. "He was a good father to me."

"My wife died at just about that time," Graham continued with his story. "I tried even harder to find your mother and you. I looked everywhere. You can't know how hard I tried to find the two of you. But I finally came to the conclusion that, not finding you, was my punishment for what I had done. That's when I gave up the search."

Holly was shaken by his words. How he must have suffered. She could imagine what he, as well as her mother, had gone through. She and Michael had arrived at just about this same point when Graham came along to make his unexpected disclosure.

It suddenly occurred to Holly that this news changed everything. It had taken her until this very moment to realize what it meant. She was now allowed to love Michael, without boundaries.

Michael had remained standing near the door, realizing that this was something between Graham and Holly, something he had no right to interrupt, even though the other man had invited him to be there. He had grasped the implication of Graham's news a few minutes sooner than Holly who was now looking at him with shining eyes, not from tears, this time, but from sheer happiness.

With the news out in the open, and apparently all of it told, Michael stepped forward. When he was standing in front of the older man, he first bowed his head, and then, looking at Graham, said very formally, "May I ask permission to marry your daughter?"

Willard Graham laughed out loud. All the tension was gone from his face. "You sure don't waste time, young man, but I can't think of anyone I'd rather have for a son-in-law. However, I do have one request. Since you will have her for the rest of your life, I would like to take Holly home with me until the wedding. That way we can, at least in a small measure, make up for some of the time we've lost."

A Mother's Sins

Chapter 27

It was a wonderfully warm autumn day when Michael and Holly were united in marriage in a small chapel partially hidden under the oaks on the manor grounds. Willard Graham watched the young couple with mixed feelings as they were raptly listening to the pastor's words, and he couldn't prevent the tears that welled up in his eyes. He was sad to have lost Holly's company so soon after he'd found her, but he was glad at her happiness. At any rate, they could visit each other often. And, perhaps there would soon be some grandchildren to boast about.

With his thoughts getting a little ahead of him as he was contemplating the future, he came back to the present when his daydreams were interrupted by a loud sob from Gertrude who was sitting next to him. Not quite sure whether the housekeeper's tears were based on her happiness over the young couple's marriage or by the recent loss of her employer, Graham patted her leg awkwardly, trying to calm her down.

Holly and Michael were exchanging rings just then. A few minutes later, they left the little chapel side by side and there was no mistaking the happiness the two young people were experiencing.

Richard Storm was one of the first to congratulate the newlyweds.

"The worst day of my life," he whispered in the young bride's ear.

Holly laughed out loud.

"Looks to me like you replaced me in no time at all," she said eyeing his pretty receptionist who was just then congratulating Michael.

Richard nodded and grinned in response, "Sometimes fate has strange things in store for us," was his comment. "But you're right, I am not brokenhearted. I guess what I felt for you was just puppy love, although I am rather past the puppy age. But I am glad that you and Michael have found each other."

All in all, it was a splendid day, but one thing marred Holly's happiness. She was concerned about the threat Margaret O'Mally had made against the two of them so many weeks ago. She had not been able to forget that, and Michael had not been able to convince her that there was nothing to worry about in that regard. He assured her that Margaret had just spoken out of spite.

Was it then coincidence that Gertrude handed Michael an envelope on this particular day, a letter that had come all the way from Texas? Holly watched her husband tear open the envelope, assuming it was a card to congratulate them. It turned out to be a small piece of paper and Michael scanned the contents, then read the note again more slowly. Unexpectedly, with Holly watching his face closely, he broke into a big grin before he began to roar with laughter. He handed the note to Holly.

"Margaret's revenge has arrived."

Holly took the sheet of paper from his hand cautiously, as though it might burn her. A worried frown marred her brow. Soon the tenseness left her and, finally, she too started to laugh, hugging her brand-new husband who was still grinning.

Neither she nor Michael would ever be able to understand why Margaret had found it necessary to inform them that she had become engaged to a rich but elderly man. And that she was doing just fine, thank you. Michael crumpled the letter into a ball and threw it at Graham who deftly caught it. Then he took his young wife in his arms once more and twirled her around in circles while their guests watched with pleasure.

At last the two young people stopped and looked

deep into each other's eyes, forgetting, for the moment, everything and everyone around them. Only the two of them existed in that instant while their lips touched, first tenderly, then more demanding. And with that kiss, they sealed a promise to each other, to stay together for the rest of their lives.

Ursula Turner

Acknowledgements

A big thank you to all members of Night Writers who inspired me to write and write and write. And particularly to those of you who did special things for me. You know who you are! It is a pleasure knowing so many fellow writers.